Always Gardenia

Always Gardenia

A novel

BETSY HANSON

Always Gardenia is a work of fiction. Names, characters, places, and incidents are the products of the author's imagination or are used fictitiously. Any resemblance to actual events, locales, or persons, living or dead, is entirely coincidental.

Copyright © 2018 by Elizabeth L. Hanson

All rights reserved.

BRYANT
HOUSE
BOOKS

Published in the United States by Bryant House Books

Hardcover ISBN: 978-0-9998093-1-0
eBook ISBN: 978-0-9998093-2-7
Original Softcover ISBN: 978-0-9998093-3-4
Amazon KDP Softcover ISBN: 978-0-9998093-6-5

Printed in the United States of America

by Gorham Printing
Centralia, Washington

FIRST EDITION

Book design by Kathy Campbell

Cover illustration by Richard Pulkrabek

Title inspiration from Emily Painter

For Poke

Chapter One

Maybe that's Arnold Wiggens, Gardenia Pitkin thought, as the man a few yards ahead of her on the path unsnapped the leash on a copper-colored dachshund.

Checking over his shoulder first, he stooped down to harvest a jonquil from the bed where it stood sentry with dozens of others in the pale March-in-Seattle sunshine.

The man slipped the jonquil into one pocket of his navy windbreaker. From the other he pulled what looked to be tea bags, as if checking to make sure he had provisioned himself, and then slipped them back in again. No one else was treading through the campus of the University of the Northwest at eight thirty in the morning, so it *was* likely that the dachshund lover and flower plucker was Dr. Arnold Wiggens. As acting chair of the Department of English, he would make the final decision on hiring Gardenia as the administrative assistant for the department.

He could be from central casting for English professors, Gardenia thought, with his baggy khakis and rumpled curly hair and soft-soled oxfords. Even the dachshund, trotting along tetherless and veering from the path with his nose to the ground, was an appropriately eccentric accessory. I will tell him right away that we share a fondness for dachshunds, though my Susie is of miniature lineage and his fellow, a noble standard.

With a crisp whistle, must-be-Dr.-Wiggens beckoned the dog and snapped on the leash before unlocking the door to the Arts and Sciences Building.

"Excuse me," she called as she hurried to the entrance. "I'm Gardenia Pitkin!"

Hearing her name hang in the morning quiet, Gardenia felt her cheeks flush. Well, what if this *isn't* Arnold Wiggens? What if this is someone who has no reason to know my name at all, a denizen of the philosophy department or a visiting Bulgarian historian or even . . . a custodian?

But the man turned and smiled.

"Ah, a timely arrival indeed. I forgot to mention in my email that the building would be locked because of spring break." He extended his hand. "Arnold Wiggens, acting chair, taking over for Dr. Gludger. Thank you for agreeing to meet me at this early hour."

"No problem. And this is?" Gardenia knelt and offered her fist for the dachshund to sniff.

"Leroy. Well behaved enough to be my office mate. Dog dander is never a problem. Dachshunds are well known for their hypoallergenic qualities."

"I know. I have a dachshund too. Though she's a cross between a longhaired and a wirehaired. Scruffy and smaller, but still a dachshund."

Arnold Wiggens smiled, showing slightly prominent teeth. "We already have something in common. We'll take the stairs, if you don't mind. We're on the second floor."

He picked Leroy up, carefully supporting the dog's hindquarters and thus certifying him as one who knew the fragility of the lowrider back. Gardenia had hoped to have a chance to dodge into the restroom to brush her hair and re-gloss her lips before her appointment, but she sensed that Dr. Wiggens would not notice, nor care, about such last-minute primping.

He unlocked one of the wide French doors leading to the English department. From one of the back offices came the drone of a female voice.

"Ah, it must be our esteemed poetry professor, Frieda Hamm. One of the few who can't refrain from working, even during spring break. Hello, Wiggens here!" he called. When there was no response, he whispered to Gardenia, "Indeed, the mesmerizing qualities of John Donne. May I ask you to wait a moment while I get the good fellow settled?"

"Of course." Gardenia sat in a chair near what appeared to be the desk for the administrative assistant and with a clear view of Arnold Wiggens's office. She watched as he coaxed the purloined jonquil into a thin-necked white vase on his office windowsill and filled Leroy's food bowl from a bag of kibble in the bottom drawer of the file cabinet. Gardenia had not noticed whether he wore a wedding ring, but she would put money on the notion that he was a childless bachelor, though why she concluded such a thing, she wasn't sure. Maybe it was the way he treated Leroy, as if a child substitute, or perhaps his styleless jacket and trousers. A good wife would have insisted that he put on "nicer" things for a first meeting with a potential employee.

I used to give Torre editorial comments on his clothes, Gardenia recalled, on days when he was lost in his math-teacher concerns and didn't realize that he had a dab of teriyaki sauce on his shirt or that he'd worn the same cords four days in a row.

The droning had stopped. A small, sturdy pony of a woman, in jeans and a brown sweatshirt, emerged from one of the back offices, leading a taller, younger woman who seemed to be the exact opposite appearance-wise, with her straight planks of white-blonde hair, trim red jacket, and long legs in slender black trousers.

"Where's Dr. Wiggens?" the sturdy pony asked. "We've been waiting for him."

"In his office." Gardenia stood up and extended her hand. "I'm Gardenia Pitkin. I'm interviewing for the administrative assistant job."

"Frieda Hamm. I teach poetry. Or should I say, *about* poetry. And poets. None of those workshops, like the others do." Her adamant tone indicated that this was something she was either proud of or expected she would have to defend.

"And *I* am Laurel DuBarr." The blonde shook Gardenia's hand.

"*Dr.* DuBarr," Frieda said. "She's the new post-modern adjunct. For just this quarter. Where's Arn?"

He stepped out of his office.

"Arnold Wiggens, Chaucer specialist and acting chair." With a quick bow he offered his hand, which Dr. DuBarr shook with authority.

"I thought you said eight fifteen. Or maybe I entered it in my calendar wrong. The door to the building was locked, but fortunately Frieda had just arrived and let me in." Dr. DuBarr pulled on a silver hoop earring.

"My apologies," Dr. Wiggens said.

"I told her to look around while I did my early-morning reciting," Frieda said. "Excuse me, but some of us don't take much of a vacation. I have to get back to my lesson plans."

"Thanks for letting me in," Dr. DuBarr said, and Frieda called "No worries!" as she headed back to her office.

"We're lucky to have you on short notice, what with Dr. Gludger suddenly deciding to retire after his heart-attack scare." Arnold jammed his hands into the pockets of his khakis. "I hope you have had enough time to prepare for your classes?"

At this Dr. DuBarr tossed her hair and fiddled again with the silver hoop. "I have had almost *no* time to prepare."

"Indeed. My apologies." Arnold raked his tangle of graying auburn curls.

For the second time in about half a minute you've apologized to her, and now you're even blushing, Gardenia thought. And *she* is the new hire who should be deferential to *you*.

"Never mind," Dr. DuBarr said. "I'd like to see my office."

"Indeed. Right away." Dr. Wiggens turned to Gardenia. "Would you like to join us? A tour of the premises?"

"Sure."

Leading Dr. DuBarr down the hall, Arnold patted the windbreaker pocket that held the tea bags. This sleek young lady wouldn't appreciate a mug of tea, Gardenia thought. More the espresso macchiato type.

"This is the office of Dr. Gludger, now happily living in, we hope, heart-healthy retirement on Lopez Island," Arnold said as he opened a door at the far end of the hallway. "One of the few offices with two sets of windows."

Dr. DuBarr strode into Dr. Gludger's office, with its lonely landscape of empty bookcases and denuded desktop, and strode right out again.

"He smoked, didn't he?"

"Dr. Gludger did go outside to the service entrance to have a cigarette. But the entire building is smoke-free," Dr. Wiggens said.

"It doesn't matter. It comes in with them on their clothes. Can't you smell it?"

"It's not too bad," Gardenia said, even though she had noticed the odor as soon as Dr. Wiggens had opened the door.

"No one told me I would have an office that smells of cigarette smoke. Is there another one I could use?"

"Unfortunately, 'The inn is full,' you might say," Dr. Wiggens said.

At this Dr. DuBarr plunked her leather satchel on the desk and knelt down to sniff the carpet. "The stink has soaked into the carpet. Can you arrange to have it replaced?"

"*Replaced?* Ah. As I recall, there is a facilities budget. I can investigate the available sums." From his non-tea-bag-holding windbreaker pocket, Dr. Wiggens dug out a small notebook and stub of a pencil and scribbled something with a flourish. "I'll discuss this with Hamilton Dodge, the dean of Arts and Sciences. I believe you met him when you interviewed?"

Dr. DuBarr stood up and adjusted the waistband of her slacks, not replying to the question. "Hate to be a complainer on my first day"—about time you realized how demanding you're being, Gardenia thought—"but it makes no sense to set up my office until that odor is gone. I'll go home and work there today, Dr. Wigham."

"*Wiggens*," he peeped. "But do call me Arnold."

"Oops. OK, Arn. Thanks for your trouble."

A miasma of flowery scent wafted around Dr. DuBarr as she passed Gardenia on the way to the door. Not appropriate for an academic setting, Gardenia thought, but it does explain why she is so touchy about the smell of an office carpet.

"We're lucky to have Dr. DuBarr, an instructor of such stellar credentials," Dr. Wiggens said to Gardenia. "But now, about your position. I can't say that it is the most scintillating work in the world, but we generally don't bother the secretary—er, the *administrative assistant*—too much. The odd copying job, maybe a letter of recommendation. Students coming in with drop/add forms. And the ones who are in tears over an A minus and want to know if they can get a grade change."

"I have a son a few years older than these students," Gardenia said, "so I know the age group. Quite like it. And the office is pleasant."

"As far as I'm concerned, the final interview is hereby finished. You are duly employed." He shook her hand and pulled the tea bags from his pocket. "May I offer you a cup of Keemun?"

"Yes, please."

"Sugar? Milk?"

"Milk, please."

Arnold loped down the hall to the department's kitchenette, holding the tea bags by their strings, one in each hand, as if taking them for a walk.

I'll suggest renting one of those carpet cleaners, Gardenia thought, and I can show him how to use it. Not in my job description, but I'm betting that the "facilities budget" is for paper clips and copy paper and other dribs and drabs, not a new carpet. It's clear that Dr. Wiggens, whatever his relationship status may be, is no match for the requests of a young female professor who could easily be featured on a billboard for Icelandic Air.

Gardenia zipped her parka against the chill of the early-spring evening as she cut a path around a spray of broken beer bottles. Three winos hunched together near the totem pole in Pioneer Square. When she and Torre had first moved to Seattle nearly thirty years before, they had often made an outing to the Pioneer Square neighborhood, for Saturday breakfast at a bakery café, several hours of browsing at the Elliott Bay Book Company, and visits to the galleries housed in the renovated historic brick buildings near Occidental Park.

But the bookstore had moved to Capitol Hill, and the bakery had competition from cafés in every other Seattle neighborhood. The restaurants that remained catered to sports fans before and after games at the nearby stadiums or gallerygoers out for the first-Thursday art walks. Otherwise this part of the city was known mainly for the sad drunks and vagabonds who were passing time until they could check into the nearby mission lodgings.

"Have a nice evening, lady," one of the winos said.

Without thinking Gardenia waved feebly, surprised to see that the youngest drunk looked to be about the same age as her only child, twenty-four-year-old Hans.

"You look like a nice lady. Hey, Nice Lady. Can you spare some change? Hard times around here."

Gardenia felt for some coins in her parka pocket, changed her mind, and hurried across the street. What was the use of giving the young fellow money? He would spend any handouts on more of the proverbial hair of the dog. But her maternal instinct clanged like a gong. How did it happen that sweet, innocent boys became drunken, defeated men? Life was not particularly easy for Hans right now. Maybe the day would come when he would drown his sorrows, lose his bearings, and end up beckoning to other boys' mothers and begging for change.

"Fuck you then, Nice Lady!" the young man yelled. "Fuckin' Nice Lady!"

Gardenia picked up her pace. She was glad she was wearing her comfortable black loafers in case she needed to run, though she guessed that none of those drunks had the stamina for the chase. I'll send a check to the mission, she thought, or the local food bank, but she wondered if she would. There were so many other tugs on the little money she had.

"Hey there, girlfriend!"

Sylvie Grant picked her way across the cobblestone plaza in her high-heeled boots, her leather blazer buttoned to frame her slender waist.

"I'll never get used to the winos around here." Gardenia embraced her longtime friend. "Art galleries in historic buildings and the homeless. One of those drunks is about Hans's age."

"It *is* sad." Sylvie pulled a glossy gallery guide from her shoulder bag and held it out to Gardenia. "But we're not here to solve the world's problems. It's a night out for you. See some paintings, the special spring art walk. Maybe meet some new people."

Sylvie looked Gardenia up and down, intending perhaps to be subtle but not succeeding.

"It got chilly after the sun went down, so I put on my winter parka." Gardenia regretted this defensive comment as soon as the words were out of her mouth. The parka had been a gift from Torre, and she'd wear it whenever she could, thank you very much! It wasn't exactly the way the chic dressed when they were out for the evening at art galleries, but she didn't care. Her eyes pricked with tears as she remembered

Torre presenting her, one Saturday afternoon years ago, with a large REI shopping bag that held the new parka.

"Never mind, you look fine," Sylvie said. "But hey, what about the job?"

"I met the department chair this morning, and he said I am 'duly employed.' I start tomorrow morning."

"Denie, that's great. Yay! What's he like?"

"He seems nice enough. He brings a dachshund to work. Looks like he's from central casting for English professors. He has this stilted way of talking, like an Edwardian vicar. But overall, not the bossy type, I'd say." Gardenia was sure that Dr. Wiggens had not an overbearing bone in his body. He had carefully handed her a mug of strong black tea and gestured vaguely at the administrative assistant's desk, inviting her to take over. "It's been a long day. I'm going to get a coffee before I do the gallery thing. Go ahead. I'll catch up."

Gardenia carried her decaf latte to the one empty table in Café Venezia. Across from her sat two young couples about Hans's age, chatting and laughing without, it seemed, a care in the world, so unlike her poor boy. I'll offer to baby-sit so Hans and Caitlin can do the gallery walk next month, she thought. I'll slip him a twenty for dessert and coffee for the two of them.

On her phone she clicked on the most recent photo of Milo, riding on his daddy's shoulders, and scrolled through the older shots of her grandson. Why had she thought him so amazing when he was a baby and a one-year-old, now that he was a fully functioning eighteen months with a vocabulary that expanded by the day and a confident toddler's gait?

The most adorable little boy in the world, Milo was born just six months after his grandfather Torre had died.

"May I share your table?"

"Oh, of course." Gardenia wrestled her chunky parka off the extra chair and shoved her ceramic latte cup aside to make room for the dark-haired man's tiny espresso cup and a plate with a small lemon tart.

You couldn't say no if someone asked to share your table when it was this crowded, but she felt self-conscious sitting across from this attractive fellow, who seemed about her age, with swatches of silver at his temples.

"Lex Ohashi." He held out his hand.

"Gardenia Pitkin." One of his front teeth had a small chip. Odd, in this day of sophisticated dentistry, she thought, that a clean-shaven middle-aged man wearing a white shirt and black V-neck sweater would not have his tooth fixed. On the other hand, it added a certain boyish charm to his smile. His slender ring finger was bare.

Lex folded his black scarf as if it were cashmere origami, and with a small Swiss Army knife, he cut the lemon tart carefully into four pieces and extended the plate to her. "Would you like some?"

"No thank you."

"You said your name is *Gardenia*? Let me guess. You wanted to be a *Jennifer* or *Julie* when you were a kid?"

"I did."

"Well, let's consider *Lester*. Named after my mom's dad. The other grandfather was born in Japan, but they decided not to call me Kiyoshi or some such. Fortunately in first grade a kid started calling me Lex, for which I am eternally grateful. Though the kid was a bully. Do you come to Pioneer Square often?"

"I used to years ago, with my husband, for the first-Thursday art walks. But this is the first time I've been to the galleries since he died.

My friend wanted me to join her. The galleries are staying open tonight to welcome spring, or something."

Why don't I just spread it *all* out on this little round café table? Gardenia thought. Tell this handsome stranger all the basic facts?

I, Gardenia Pitkin, am a bereft fifty-six-year-old widow who wakes up with a start every morning and reaches for her husband's large, warm back, only to find cold sheets.

Who eats a salad and a bowl of soup alone at her kitchen table most nights.

Who sometimes drinks a couple of glasses of wine while she watches DVDs, just because the alcohol helps.

Who has a son and a grandson but whose husband, whom she loved so much, is dead, dead, dead.

Lex leaned forward. "I am sorry for your loss."

"Heart attack. Very sudden. And he even rode his bike every day." Gardenia stuffed her napkin into her empty latte cup and slipped the cup into the dirty-dishes bin behind her. She started to put on the well-worn parka but changed her mind, draping it clumsily over her arm instead.

"Thank you for sharing your table. I'm sorry we didn't get to chat more." Lex stood up, a suave touch that would have eluded even kindhearted Torre.

"You're welcome," Gardenia said. "Have a nice evening."

AT THE GUNDERSON Gallery, Sylvie was studying a large painting of a sea anemone. The other gallerygoers were dressed mostly in black, though there were those in down vests or REI parkas not unlike Gardenia's, typical of the carefree sartorial culture of Seattle.

"I thought you were going to get coffee?" Sylvie said.

"I did," Gardenia said.

"Oh, it looks like you just had a stiff drink or two. Your cheeks are bright red."

"All I had was a decaf latte, but it was stuffy in the café." Gardenia patted her warm face. I should be in tears now, she thought, having just talked to that Lex about Torre's death, but her eyes were dry, as if she had finally begun to use up the groundwater of her grief.

The broad window of the gallery framed Lex as he left Café Venezia, twined the cashmere muffler around his neck, and sauntered toward a parking lot across from the winos' hangout.

A pleasant man, but I'll never see him again, Gardenia thought, and so what if I don't? I'm not interested in meeting new people, no matter what Sylvie says.

So that is that.

Chapter Two

HAMILTON DODGE, DEAN of the School of Arts and Sciences, was hoisting a pair of small yellow dumbbells. A black beret covered his bald pate, and his Hawaiian aloha shirt was unbuttoned, revealing a white tank-style T-shirt.

Arnold had heard that these undershirts were called wifebeaters, which he certainly hoped Dean Dodge was not.

"A new carpet?" Dean Dodge said. "Good God, man, when your department is fighting over how to pay for the copy machine and paper clips?"

"Dr. DuBarr referred to the health hazards of secondhand smoke," Arnold said. Well, those had not been her precise words, but couldn't one extrapolate from her intense reaction as she knelt to inspect the smoke-infused carpet?

"I didn't promise her a rose garden, as they say. Not an easy trick these days, to score a temporary English position, with the good chance of it becoming permanent. I would think she could *deal*." Dodge lowered the dumbbells to the desk and stretched his arms as if he were a sinner at a revival meeting. "Wiggens, you could keep a set of weights in the office like I do, so you wouldn't have to make time to go to the gym."

"I walk to work," Arnold said, immediately wishing that he hadn't.

"Only counts if you keep up the pace," Dodge said.

"I beg your pardon?"

"Walking to work. All well and good, but at our age you've got to push your heart rate up. And do the strength training." He swigged from a stainless-steel water bottle as he splayed himself in his leather desk chair, a slim stripe of perspiration marking the front of the wife-beater.

Arnold was not as concerned about rippling biceps as Dodge was, but what right, he wondered, did a dean have to lecture a faculty member on physical fitness?

Dodge had good reason to work out, married as he was to a woman many years younger. Mrs. Dodge's photo simpered in a frame on her husband's desk. She was a nurse from some Asian country—though Arnold couldn't remember which. Thailand? The Philippines? The dean had been quick to clarify, after they were married, that she was not an online bride but instead a nurse and bona fide American citizen.

What Dodge had *not* mentioned was that the two met after he had hired her as a home-care nurse for the first Mrs. Dodge, who was recuperating from a long cancer treatment.

"He may be our dean, but I can never respect him again after what he did to his wife," Frieda Hamm had sniffed to Arnold when the news of Dodge's divorce and subsequent marriage had percolated through the four floors of the Arts and Sciences Building. "Imagine surviving that horrible illness and when you finally go into remission, your husband is in bed with the woman who helped you to and from the bathroom."

Frieda's description brought to mind Hamilton Dodge and the nurse cavorting on a hospital bed while the ailing wife was marooned in the bathtub.

Maybe Hamilton Dodge's wife had been a terror, and he was planning to file for divorce but had to put off the legal machinations when she got sick. The sultry nurse had happened along at what was either a good or bad time, Arnold supposed, depending on the part one might be playing in the drama.

Marriages were always fifty-fifty, but you typically get to hear only half the story, as Arnold's mother, the estimable Dorothy Wiggens, noted anytime there was news of a couple breaking up or a spouse philandering. In his own admittedly unsuccessful experience with women, Arnold had to agree that this was true, despite Frieda's outrage.

"I suppose I could trade offices with her," Arnold said to Dodge.

"*Trade offices?*"

"With Dr. DuBarr. I found the smoke odor all but imperceptible."

"Oh yes, back to the carpet. No, I can't imagine faculty members moving offices just days before classes start. Too much commotion for your colleagues. They're all running scared to get ready for the quarter. And guess who would hear all the complaints about noise and clutter and so on?"

Arnold resisted mentioning that the only English professor who had shown up that week before classes was the murmuring Frieda Hamm. "I suppose I could manage the move on Sunday."

"No, no, sets a bad precedent," Dodge insisted. "People are testy about their offices. Territorial instincts and all that. Two people trade, then someone else wants to, and the other person doesn't. Pretty soon you've got yourself a royal mess. And Dr. DuBarr should consider herself lucky to have that corner office. Windows on two sides! I'm sure you can convince her to accept the situation. The old Chaucer charm, eh?"

Dodge chuckled at his own quip, though Arnold had no idea what coaxing a slender blonde into accepting a fetid carpet had to do with Geoffrey Chaucer, a man who deserved reverence and reverence only.

"And speaking of Chaucer, you were going to keep me posted on the status of that manuscript."

"Out and about, one might say." Arnold hoped that the heat he felt in his cheeks might somehow not look like a sheepish blush.

"No takers?"

"Interest has been noted but nothing definitive." This meant that in December Yale had acknowledged receipt of his query. "*Pacing the Story: Geoffrey Chaucer's Dramatic Constructions in 'The Canterbury Tales,'*" Arnold said.

"Can't help but think you're going to have a hard slog, getting that published," Dodge said. "University publishers need sexier topics these days. The powers that be are rumbling about the faculty publishing as much as possible. And tenured folk have to keep at it or risk having their classes eliminated." Dodge leaned down to shove the dumbbells under his desk.

"Anyone who has ever generated a manuscript understands how arduous it can be to find a publisher."

"Why not ask our esteemed new professor, Dr. DuBarr, about her publishers? She has at least one book, you know."

"A good idea." It was touchy, asking a colleague for the so-called good word to an editor. And Dr. DuBarr might ask to review his manuscript first, a thought that made him feel uncomfortable, though it was a solid piece of work that he was ready to share with anyone.

Dodge said, "By the way—air freshener?"

And those words were, Arnold thought, the most useful that the dean had ever spoken in his presence, offering a solution to the stinky office of Robert Gludger. Hearing this suggestion was almost worth the minuet of warning and humiliation he had danced for a few minutes as Dodge had quizzed him on his unpublished book.

⁓

ON FRIDAY MORNING Arnold struggled to turn the key in the lock of his office door as he gripped Leroy's leash and a canvas grocery bag with his left hand, a thermos of milky Keemun tucked under his right arm. As the dachshund jerked on the leash, impatient to get inside and gobble his morning scoop of kibble, the contents of the bag tumbled onto the floor.

"Let me help you with that," Gardenia offered.

"Oh! Much obliged, but I can manage," he said, but Gardenia nonetheless gathered up the three air fresheners: Hint o' Heather, Lavender Cloud, and Aroma Dulce.

It had been so many weeks since the former administrative assistant, Doris Breen, had quit the university for the delights of inheritance-financed cruises, Arnold was surprised to see her desk occupied. He had forgotten that the new assistant with the flower name—*Magnolia? Lily?* Ah, *Gardenia*—would be starting that morning.

As she smiled Arnold noted her dark brown eyes and the decided gap between her front teeth, featured also in the smiles of some famous movie actresses and Chaucer's Wife of Bath—though this new administrative assistant bore no further resemblance to that bawdy lady.

"Dean Dodge said these might get rid of the cigarette odor in Gludger's office," Arnold said.

Gardenia knelt beside Leroy and rubbed the bliss spots at his temples. "Opening the windows might help. I don't think Aroma Dulce is going to do the trick. My opinion, but those deodorizers are almost as bad as what they're trying to cover up. You may have to get one of those machines that shampoo the carpet. My husband and I used to rent one from the Safeway."

Why did I think that Hamilton Dodge knew what he was talking about when he had hissed slyly "Air fresheners"? Arnold asked himself. He rarely thought that anything Dodge said was particularly intelligent. Yet there the man was, pumping iron in his large, airy dean's office, with a photo of a pretty young wife on his desk and an ample salary plopped into his bank account every month.

"I know nothing about carpet cleaning," Arnold ventured. "But I'd be happy to pay you for your time if you and your husband would show me."

"My husband is dead."

"Oh, I beg your pardon. I am so sorry. My sincerest condolences."

"That's OK. You had no way of knowing." She kissed Leroy's forehead. "I'm used to it. You learn that the grapevine doesn't twine around to everybody who's ever known you. Amazing, the people who missed the news. Moms you knew back in the preschool days. Or from swimming lessons. Anyway, if you'd like me to show you how to use one of the cleaners, I could do that. Maybe Sunday morning?"

"But imposing on your weekend..."

"It's OK. It won't take long for you to get the hang of it."

"I'm most grateful."

I should have asked Dr. DuBarr to help, Arnold thought, although that would not be the usual way of welcoming someone new to the department. Or I could have asked that she hire someone to clean the carpet.

Ah well, consider it *outflow*, he told himself, a term favored by his good-hearted mother, who believed in always giving more than you have to.

Gardenia must be another *outflow-er*, he thought, since she had offered to join him in this thankless task. With her help, the office would be sweet smelling and ready for Dr. DuBarr's books and wall decorations by Monday. I shall refer to it as "de-Gludgered," which our new adjunct will find amusing.

"SOMETHING FROM YOUR high school reunion committee," Dorothy Wiggens said, handing her son an envelope that evening. "They send things to the parents' address, which is odd, considering how many of us are probably dead. Or gone off our heads in a nursing home somewhere."

"Yet here you are, full of vim and vigor." Arnold put his arm around his mother's wiry shoulders.

"Piss and vinegar would be more like it."

"Not the words I would use in my mother's presence, but since you did, I agree." Inside the envelope was a densely typed, single-spaced letter. "Ah, our thirtieth high school reunion. Only the bravehearted, who have not added adipose or lost their hair, would dare to show up."

"They say people see an old crush at a high school reunion and *whammo*. Could be an ideal place to meet someone. Shared background, you know." Dorothy lifted Leroy up to nestle on the sofa beside her and pulled a library DVD from the stack on the side table.

"Abscond with one of the lonely hearts. Or one of the former cheerleaders, twice divorced and gone to fat."

"Arnold, you know what I mean. It couldn't hurt."

"Tsk-tsk. You agreed to give up the matchmaking." Here was his chance. "But, as a matter of fact, I met two new women in one day."

Dorothy sat up straight, jostling Leroy out of his preferred position of leaning against her, chin on her lap. "Two? Well, there's some good news!"

"One's a temporary faculty member, the other our kind and efficient new administrative assistant."

"They are about your age? And single?"

"Within a range of my age. And both single." At least he was assuming this was the case with Dr. DuBarr.

At this Dorothy stood up and embraced her only son. "I am so glad that you are open to meeting women. You are still young! And have a good job. And most of your hair. Which one will you ask out first?"

"Neither, because both of them are colleagues. Not OK to meet them outside the department." Which may or may not be true, Arnold thought.

"Oh fiddle," Dorothy said. "What's wrong with falling in love with another professor?"

"I'll portion out the Chocolate Chorale while you cue up the Miss Marple." Serving ice cream gave him a reason to dodge into the kitchen and thus remove himself from the subject of Arnold and Available

Women. Fie on me for thinking the quip about two women in one day would not snag me in the uncomfortable discussion about how I might meet someone, he thought.

And since when did he want to "meet someone" anyway? Laurel DuBarr, he admitted, he found attractive. Gardenia Pitkin, though clearly one of those Good People that he fortunately had met in different situations throughout his life, was a widow, no doubt still grieving. Already she had impressed him with her generosity about the carpet and with her love of dachshunds, but beyond that, he had no thoughts about her at all.

Arnold settled into the sagging easy chair with his bowl of ice cream, grateful for the DVDs of Agatha Christie mysteries that gave him something companionable to do with his mother without having to think of things to talk about.

"The clothes the women wore. All those little hats. I had one sort of like that." Dorothy dislodged Leroy to get up and touch, on the screen, a cloche adorned with a feather. "Cost me half my wages from the dime store. But I felt so grown-up."

"The chapeau era. When did it end, exactly?"

"Oh lordy, who knows. But good riddance. All that money spent on something to stick on your head." She smoothed her black knit pants. Years before, she had given up skirts, though he remembered clinging to them as a small child, his face pressed into the supple, fragrant fabric.

"You're sure they're both single?" Dorothy said two-thirds of the way through the episode.

"Pardon?"

"The two new women. The professor and the secretary. I'd say the professor is more likely for you."

"Mother, that's enough."

The sudden revelation of who had committed the murder in the vicarage distracted Dorothy. Arnold returned their empty ice-cream bowls to the kitchen and fetched his jacket.

"Time for me to go," he said.

"So soon? Well, it's the beginning of the quarter, and I know you are always so busy and need to get a good night's sleep. Call me when you get back to your apartment."

"As always, Mumsie." Arnold kissed his mother's thin pleated cheek and handed her a glass of water and the vials of her evening vitamins and statin medication.

What sort of films does Dr. DuBarr prefer? he wondered as he drove home. Not Miss Marple. Chilly Swedish ones? Moody French? He hoped she wasn't a fan of the slick Hollywood claptrap that was played in the multiplexes. He would check the listings for the local film societies and invite her to see something with him. This would offer a chance, afterward, to use the film's theme as the start of a discussion about their academic interests. He would ask questions regarding po-mo and how it might relate to Chaucer's work.

He didn't even know if Laurel was "available." She wore no wedding ring, but that did not mean she wasn't harboring a swarthy sculptor in her apartment, or a patent attorney with a sleek red sports car and a penchant for surprising her with weekends in the San Juans or even Hawaii. But how was he to determine the details of her personal life, short of asking her directly?

Thirty years ago, in high school, he recalled Jennifer Langley asking him in algebra class if Tony Caletti, his next-door neighbor, was "going with" anyone. Arnold had told her that as far as he knew, he wasn't. Not long after, he had seen Jennifer picking Tony up to go to the Sadie Hawkins dance.

He could revive the secondary-school tactic of asking a third party about another's love life. But who, in this case, would that person be?

Ah, but of course.

Gardenia.

Chapter Three

HANS PITKIN OPENED the front door of the Ballard townhouse, Milo in his arms.

"My darlings!" Gardenia set her gift of potted purple tulips on the dusty front porch and hugged both of them. "You can leave these out here or take them inside, whichever. They'll last longer than a bouquet."

"Thanks, Mom," Hans said, "and thanks for coming over on short notice, after your first day of work and all. Caitlin's girlfriends wanted her to go out for drinks. It's the last Friday night before classes start next week."

"No problem. You know you and Milo make my day. Any day. Anytime."

Even if I am the backup plan that makes it possible for the selfish Caitlin to do whatever she wants, Gardenia thought, but she decided to let her peevish feelings about her daughter-in-law slide so she could enjoy her "boys" instead.

"Oh, you smell so good, so good." Gardenia nuzzled Milo's soft neck like a mare with her foal.

"Really?" Hans said. "He needs a new diaper. Uh, if you wouldn't mind? I have to get ready for work."

"Grandmothers have a forgiving sense of smell. I'll take care of him."

While Hans bounded up the narrow stairs to the second floor, Gardenia slipped Milo down to stand on the cream-colored carpet and stepped out of her worn brown clogs. Milo's tiny sneakers sat between Caitlin's shiny gold-colored flats and Hans's low hikers. Caitlin—or Hans?—had been smart to declare their home a no-shoe zone from the beginning, to protect the pale carpet. You had to wonder what the developers were thinking, installing a nearly white wall-to-wall.

But wait. Caitlin's father, Stan Curlew, had bought the place for them before it was finished, so maybe Caitlin had chosen the color? She must have seen a similar carpet in some glossy home décor magazine and insisted that they have the same, one of those battles that Hans had chosen not to fight.

Milo settled happily into his booster seat after Gardenia had changed him. From the fridge she extracted some applesauce and a tiny container of yogurt, the kind marketed for babies but nonetheless full of sugar. In a bowl by the sink was one greenish banana.

"Mom, Caitlin said you could heat up some SpaghettiOs for him. He always eats those. Or there's some leftover pizza. He even likes the olives." Hans, showered and shaved, looked more like a twenty-four-year-old dude and less like the overworked young father that he was.

Gardenia had already decided that Milo would *not* have SpaghettiOs or cold pizza for dinner. She'd see if there were a few eggs and cheese for a small omelet. She sliced the banana into chunks for the toddler.

"Too bad you have to do the night shift at the co-op," Gardenia said.

"Caity decided she wants to do day classes this quarter." He stuck a flabby piece of pizza in the microwave. "I'm lucky the manager had a shift for me right away. Otherwise we'd have to find childcare, quick, and that's mucho bucks. Hey, I forgot to ask. How's the new job?" The pizza he finished in three bites, washing it down with tap water from one of Milo's robot-decorated plastic cups.

"First day, so I can't say much. The acting chair seems eccentric, but he brings his standard in with him to work."

"*Standard,* as in *dachshund*? Sweet. Something in common."

"I'm so used to miniature Susie. It's been years since I've seen a full-sized dachshund. Took me right back to my childhood, when we had Lucy." Gardenia helped herself to one of the two last pieces of pizza.

"Cool. Listen, Mom, I'd love to hear more about your job and everything, but I'm going to be late. I'll be back after eleven. Go ahead and nap on the couch."

"Wait, Caitlin won't be home by then?"

"Not sure. Her night out with the girls."

"You get a chance to go out with your buddies?" she called as Hans headed for the front door.

"Naw, not right now, too much other stuff going on."

His Toyota wagon rumbled a noisy exit from the parking place in front of the townhouse. A bad muffler? When she and Torre were first married, with no savings or credit cards for sudden car repairs, their clunker's rasping muffler had announced their poverty to all of the world.

Daddy Curlew would be all over the Toyota's repair issue, though, just as he had been in buying a townhouse for the little family after Milo was born. The elephantine sofa and the supersized TV were from Daddy Curlew. Hans must have hated his father-in-law's handouts.

Torre had been embarrassed when Gardenia's parents had slipped her a check for that muffler, and another for Hans's first piano lessons, and yet another when she had miscarried their second child just as Torre changed jobs and there was a gap in their health insurance.

"Thank you, dear Mom and Dad," Gardenia said, looking up at the ceiling, as this was in the general direction of Heaven—well, who could say that there was no such place and that her deceased parents were not enjoying an afterlife there? I'm not a believer, she thought, except when it makes me feel better to imagine that I will join them, and Torre, someday. Torre had always enjoyed her parents' cocktail-hour tradition, so maybe the three of them were laughing and chatting and sipping margaritas together by a cozy hearth somewhere in one of the "many mansions."

"Do you want to play piano?" Gardenia asked when Milo had finished his banana and a last fistful of cheesy eggs. At least Caitlin was not the most observant person in the world, saying nothing if you got a new haircut or glasses or painted a room in your house, so she was unlikely to notice that the rack on the refrigerator door was two eggs shy and that the can of SpaghettiOs was collecting dust on the shelf.

"Pa-no!" Milo raced over and reached up for the keys of the old dark-wood upright that had once stood in Gardenia's living room.

"That old thing?" Caitlin had mewled the day Hans and Gardenia were discussing how to move it. "In our new house? It won't go with anything else."

"It's as important to me as . . . as . . . your scrapbooks are to you," Hans had said, straightening up. Gardenia had wanted to thump his back to congratulate him for insisting. She had always planned that he would someday have a baby grand, as his talent deserved. Instead they had paid for expensive tunings for the upright, reassured each time that this was a fine piano.

Milo pounded on the keys while Gardenia sat beside him and picked out a melody, just as she had done with Hans when he was about the same age.

She built a block tower with Milo on the impractical carpet.

She let him splash in the bathtub until the water was almost cold.

She read him some board books.

She rocked him while she gave him a bottle and sang "Good Morning Heartache" and "Baby Beluga."

When Milo finally fell asleep in his crib at eight thirty, Gardenia was exhausted.

Still, it would be two and a half hours until Hans would be home. She hoped that Susie wouldn't be too desperate to go out. Torre had always picked the little dog up and gently carried her outside rather than simply opening the back door.

The image of Torre with Susie brought familiar tears to Gardenia's eyes. "How are you, darlin'?" she called to the ceiling. "And how do you think Hans is doing, with his hectic life and the woman he married?" Maybe someday she'd get a message from Torre. Had *every* psychic throughout human history been a charlatan? Some must have been truly able to communicate with the dead. But Torre's answer about Hans would be the same as her own: Life was complicated for their son right now and would not get easier anytime soon.

"And Hans misses you, so much!"

Lose a husband, you're allowed to wallow, Gardenia thought. You even get a new label, *widow*. No word described a son who had lost his dad. Well, *fatherless,* but that was an adjective. You had to lose both parents to become a noun, an *orphan.*

But missing Torre was the least of Hans's worries. He had a child and wife to support with earnings from checking at a natural foods grocery, and an unused piano talent and an unfinished bachelor's degree—and a wife who still used her mother's credit card to buy clothes for herself and Milo and who stayed out past eleven on a Friday night with her girlfriends.

"Hi, Momma G!" Caitlin called as she opened the front door. Her heavy honey-colored hair showed beads of rain. Her red trench coat, one Gardenia had not seen before, did not have a hood, an impractical choice for Seattle. "Who put those flowers on the front porch? I didn't see them and knocked them over. Lucky I didn't hurt myself."

"I brought them, the first tulips."

"Well, thanks, but next time, could you put them somewhere out of the way?"

At this Gardenia excused herself to the bathroom at the top of the stairs, so she wouldn't say something she'd regret in response to Caitlin's rudeness. I have to watch what I say, always, Gardenia thought, if I want to keep on my daughter-in-law's good side and thus have easy access to Milo.

"Momma G, when you're finished I need to get a few things," Caitlin called from the other side of the bathroom door. "I'm in a hurry. My ride's waiting."

"A ride?" Gardenia splashed her face with cold water and dabbed it dry with the lone grayish towel.

"I just stopped by to get my stuff. I'm going to stay the night at Ashley's."

"*Stay the night?*"

"A sleepover, like the old days. We're having so much fun, we thought we'd just keep going."

"But Hans may need to sleep in tomorrow. And you have to get ready for school next week."

Gardenia loudly plopped the toilet lid down and sat.

"No big deal," Caitlin said. "I could even miss the first day or two. The syllabuses are all online."

"*Syllabi*," Gardenia growled softly.

"Um, are you almost done?"

"I'm not sure." She pulled some toilet paper noisily off the roll.

"Forget it. I'll stop at Walgreens for a toothbrush. Tell Hans to give the Miloness a kiss for me."

Caitlin's footsteps thudded heavily on the stairs. The front door slammed.

"Bitch!" The word exploded from Gardenia as if it had been loaded and ready for hours. Days. *Years*. Her exquisite son, saddled with this selfish creature. Her exquisite grandson, with this lackadaisical mother. And was she *really* staying with Ashley or instead, shacking up with some rich lover-boy?

Torre would have scolded her for this suspicion. "When you hear hoofbeats, think horses, not zebras," he'd often said, and he had always been right. The likely thing in most situations was the most mundane. No need to jump on the Catastrophe Wagon.

Torre's sudden heart attack had been neither horse nor zebra but instead, a sudden herd of wildebeests stampeding over her life.

Caitlin is flaky, Gardenia thought, but she is also stressed, with a child and school responsibilities. She doesn't realize she is being rude to her mother-in-law.

And maybe Hans takes his stress out on Caitlin, though Gardenia couldn't imagine her son as anything but a good husband. He had Torre's example, after all.

Gardenia crept into Milo's room to check on him.

He lay on his back, his arms outstretched, his fingers tucked into little fists, his white-blond bangs moist. Finally the experts had figured out that infants who sleep on their bellies were more likely to die of SIDS. How clearly she remembered thinking that if she got Hans past the SIDS age, she wouldn't have to worry about him anymore.

But this sense of security had proved to be a cruelly moving target, each age bringing new dangers and concerns. And the problems of a twenty-four-year-old child were the problems of a grown-up, much tougher than not getting invited to a birthday party or not placing in a music contest or flunking a driver's test.

The signboard at the local dry cleaners, that oracle of wisdom, had noted that week: *Industry is the enemy of melancholy*. So Gardenia washed and dried every dish on the kitchen counter and in the sink, swabbed down the crumb-splattered counters and stove top, plucked all the photos of Milo off the fridge door and wiped it off, and scraped the black crusty splatters from the bottom of the oven with a metal spatula.

With more than an hour left until Hans was due home, she moved on to the living room, dusting and organizing the stacks of Caitlin's magazines. Under an issue of *House & Garden,* she found a paper Caitlin had written for a history class about the suffragette movement. Every page had red marks, and the professor had scrawled a C-minus with the note: *Ms. Curlew, I suggest that you do some tutoring at the Writing Center. Unfortunately even a C-minus is a generous grade for this work.*

Gardenia slipped the paper back under *House & Garden.* Now she recalled a comment Hans had made long ago, when he and Caitlin had first started dating. He'd said that Caitlin was smart but had never learned to write well and didn't like to read "hard" books. Dyslexia maybe? Gardenia wondered. Well, I admire Caitlin for pursuing a degree despite her academic challenges. Would I be so determined?

She was sorting through Milo's toys and putting them in the proper bins when Hans arrived.

"Hey, Ma, it's nice enough of you to babysit—you don't have to be our cleaning lady." He hugged her.

"No problem." At least her son had the good manners to notice her effort.

"Think I'll have a beer and wait up for Caitlin."

"She didn't text you? She's staying with Ashley tonight. They decided to have a sleepover."

"Oh. Well, cool."

But Gardenia could tell from the tautness of his smile that this news didn't feel "cool."

At all.

"My poor boy," she muttered as she drove away. Poor, poor Hans, she thought. Caitlin could be *stepping out on him,* this archaic expression coming to mind as she pictured Caitlin tramping to the front door across the cream-colored carpet.

But what could she do about it?

"Nothing." Torre's remembered voice chimed the answer.

There *was* nothing she could do, nothing to protect her son from disappointment and heartbreak and betrayal, nothing as simple as easing a baby into a crib on its back to protect it from sudden tragedy.

Chapter Four

ON SUNDAY MORNING, Arnold was in the UNW parking lot, grappling with the carpet cleaner and a large jug of liquid detergent, when Gardenia's Subaru pulled up beside his Volvo station wagon.

"Just in time," she said, reaching for the jug.

"Good morning and, again, thanks for your help."

"No problem."

Leroy trotted happily beside Gardenia while Arnold trailed behind with the cumbersome carpet cleaner. She's a kind person, he thought, and sincere in her desire to help, a model for what a "good woman" is supposed to be. He would give her a small gift of thanks. But no, not a good idea. Such a token could be misconstrued as being on the sexual-harassment continuum. A pity about her husband, he thought, as Gardenia was still youngish, maybe midfifties and thus only a few years older than he.

Arnold had no way of understanding such grief, his only familial loss being the death of his father twenty-some years before. His mother had been sad, but she'd righted herself more quickly than Arnold had imagined she would, adapting to life alone and filling her days with friends and her work as a library assistant before moving to Seattle to be close to her son.

Hadn't he read somewhere that those who had been happily married often settled down with someone else soon after being widowed? It might have been the same article with alarming statistics about the likelihood of marrying at all if you had been single until a certain age. Maybe forty? He couldn't recall.

And anyone who had spent years in academia knew that no one's research was the final word on anything.

And nowhere had that article mentioned that single people could be content.

"First thing to do is open as many windows as possible," Gardenia said as she switched on the lights in Dr. DuBarr's office. "My space heater is in the car if we need it to help dry out the carpet after we clean it."

"I suppose Dr. DuBarr might have offered her husband's help." Arnold busied himself with pulling the cleaner's cord toward the outlet, pleased by how he had slipped this topic into the conversation.

"I don't think she has a husband. She doesn't wear a ring."

"Ah. A partner, then."

"Doubt she has one of those either. On Friday afternoon she dropped off a box of books and said she was glad she had found a one-bedroom apartment, since she was tired of living in a studio. No mention of any *we*."

"Ah. I say we move the chair out, and work around the desk and bookcases. I think we can get most of the carpet under the desk." I was right, Arnold thought. Gardenia is a good source of information.

She ably decanted the aqua-blue liquid into the detergent reservoir of the carpet cleaner.

"It's a pulling motion, like this." She yanked the whirring machine across a swath of carpet.

"Please, let me." Arnold was surprised at how difficult it was to drag the heavy machine across the nap of the carpet—Gardenia was stronger than she appeared.

"I never thought I would see you two here."

Frieda Hamm, in tan jeans with the cuffs rolled up and a gray sweatshirt, leaned in the doorway. She was eating a Granny Smith apple. "I thought the maintenance people did jobs like this."

"Dr. DuBarr objected to the smoke odor in Dr. Gludger's office, so Gardenia kindly offered to instruct me in the mysteries of the carpet cleaner," Arnold said.

"If you want to do my carpet, I'd love to learn how to use one of those." Frieda tossed her apple core to Leroy and peered up at Arnold, pulling gently on the sleeve of his flannel shirt.

"I'm revising my manuscript this afternoon," Arnold half lied, "so I have to head home when we're done with this."

Leroy crunched loudly on the apple core.

"Oh well, another time," Frieda said. "He likes apples, doesn't he, Arn? I remember that time we took a walk around your mother's neighborhood, he ate some of the windfalls."

"You know, Frieda, excuse us, but we do need to get this carpet taken care of," Gardenia said.

Ah, what a trustworthy ally I have in Gardenia, Arnold thought. She understands that I need rescuing from Frieda's ministrations.

"Don't you want me to throw one of my parties, for the new hires?" Frieda asked. "Everyone said they had a good time at my Christmas party last year."

"Indeed."

Gardenia said, "That's kind of you. I'd be happy to help."

"No, no, you'll be a guest of honor. Arn can pitch in. I always like to cook with my dear friends."

Arnold switched on the carpet cleaner, its domineering clamor drowning out Frieda and sending her back to her office.

By 2:00 p.m. they had gone over the carpet twice. Frieda, busy with her scans and tropes and pentameters, had stayed behind her closed office door.

"My heartiest thanks," Arnold said to Gardenia in the parking lot.

"You could have done it on your own, but it's just easier if someone shows you how. And anyway, I got to see more of Leroy." She picked the dachshund up with careful attention to supporting his hindquarters and helped him into the Volvo.

"You didn't have second thoughts about that? A Sunday morning with no one around?" Sylvie said.

"Oh come on! He's my boss. I don't think he would risk ravishing me. And wrangling a carpet cleaner is not exactly your most erotic setup." Gardenia swabbed the hummus dish with a triangle of pita.

"Sorry. I want to make sure you're safe."

These words pushed down the lever that opened the sluice for widow's tears, reminding Gardenia that she no longer had Torre for a protector. She wiped her eyes with her linen napkin.

"I'm sorry, I said the wrong thing," Sylvie said. "Stupid me."

Gardenia hated to cry. She liked to cry. She hated to have sympathy. She liked to have sympathy. She hated a considerate invitation to dinner with her happily married friend. She liked a considerate invitation to dinner with her happily married friend. Nothing was right, nothing made up for not having Torre, but something was better than nothing, until nothing seemed better than something. As if Sylvie could possibly understand, despite her gentle, generous heart.

Explaining how she felt was like trying to enlighten a celibate about the joys of sex, or explaining to a childless person the euphoria of seeing your newborn's face. If you hadn't lost a spouse, you couldn't possibly understand what kind of *hard* widowhood was.

"Cry as long as you like." Sylvie pushed her chair closer to Gardenia's so that she could hold her friend's hand.

"At least I have a job. I can check that one off my list of things to worry about at two in the morning." Gardenia was glad that Doug, Sylvie's husband, away on a business trip to Santa Fe, was not expected home that evening. That was why Sylvie had invited her over on a Sunday night. Otherwise she would have kept the end-of-the-weekend slot for a date night with her husband, just as she and Torre had done. "Anyway, it was fun to watch an Edwardian vicar handle a carpet shampooer."

Sylvie laughed, tossing her head back. "Sylvie laughs at nearly everything you say," Torre had once remarked. This was just barely an exaggeration. With Sylvie, Gardenia felt funny and clever. Torre had laughed at her jokes, and Hans did as well, though not so much recently. Her boy had so much on his mind.

Or maybe she was no longer funny to him.

"Esme thought she might be able to join us, but she texted a minute ago to say she can't," Sylvie said as she ladled some aromatic red lentil soup into two white bowls.

"Medical school must be so exhausting."

"You got that right. But she enjoys it."

The soup was rich and satisfying. The table was artful, with a small pot of primroses, white candles, a cheery Indian-print tablecloth. Sylvie's family was doing just fine, the sweet daughter Esme with a mind like a bear trap, sailing through medical school, and the kind husband, Doug, bringing home big paychecks as an accountant for a tech company. Oh man, it would be so easy to hate Sylvie for her grace and style and living, her breathing husband and her high-achieving daughter! But because her friend didn't seem to notice her own virtues, often mentioned her good luck, and didn't brag, Gardenia loved her.

"How's Milo?"

At least that's something I have that she doesn't, Gardenia thought. A beautiful grandchild.

"Adorable, as always. Getting more words. Though I know Hans was talking a blue streak when he was that age. I wrote down the words he knew when he was sixteen months old. I still have the piece of paper. I nearly filled both sides."

"They're all different. Esme didn't talk much until she was about twenty months."

And look at her now, Gardenia thought, barreling through life while my boy is soldiering along, working in a natural foods store to support his family. "Milo likes music. That's what he wanted to do after his supper, play 'pa-no.'"

"So sweet," Sylvie said. "Does Hans play much these days?"

"He said someone called him for a gig at the Jazz Bistro in Ballard last week. You know, that place that seats about forty max?"

"Cool."

Gardenia concentrated on chewing a nubbin of Sylvie's homemade artisanal bread. She didn't want to continue this line of conversation and reveal that Hans had to turn down the offer because Caitlin had planned an outing to Ikea.

Sylvie maneuvered a piece of fruit tart onto a plate for Gardenia. The luxurious strawberries were from California but hinted of early summer anyway and were sweeter than expected. Gardenia had seen cartons of them at the grocery store but couldn't afford to spend the five dollars they cost.

After the meal, she imagined flopping down on the leather sofa and pulling an afghan up to her chin, reading some of Trollope's *Barchester Towers* or watching a nature show on PBS. It would be comforting to hear Sylvie puttering around in the kitchen, as Torre often had done after dinner. But Gardenia was well mannered if nothing else, so she rinsed the white bowls and wedged them into the dishwasher, dried the wineglasses and porcelain dessert plates as Sylvie set them in the dish drainer, and wiped off the shiny granite countertops.

"We're thinking about having some people over in a few weeks. If the weather's decent, Doug's going to do something on the grill. You'll come?" Sylvie said.

"Thanks, but it depends on what's going on with Hans." Gardenia needed an excuse to decline Sylvie's invitation if she decided she couldn't handle the plunge into a group of hearty kebab-chewing married couples.

Walking Susie around the block in the dark after she returned home, Gardenia couldn't help but compare her little dachshund's hobbly gait with the pert strides of Leroy. Susie had once been that perky but now, past ten years old, had slowed down. When Hans was fourteen, they'd gone on a road trip to Montana. Each evening, as Gardenia and Torre had set up the tent, Hans had put aside his teenaged surliness and chased joyous puppy Susie around the campsite.

And who had I been back then? Gardenia asked herself. Certainly someone who would have felt perfectly happy mingling on an early-spring evening with hearty kebab-chewing married couples.

OK, I'll go to Sylvie's party, she thought. Out of my comfort zone and all that. And Torre would want me to go and have a good time, to be out in the world and "moving on," as widows are supposed to do.

Chapter Five

LATE MONDAY MORNING Laurel DuBarr was on her hands and knees again, though this time Arnold Wiggens was standing, so he saw not her back but her front as she knelt on the carpet.

"Gardenia helped," Arnold said. "We de-Gludgered the office together."

"Better." Laurel did not respond to his quip but was patting the carpet, crawling around as if searching for a contact lens. "Good, no dampness. If you don't get it dried out, you're in deep shit."

"Indeed," Arnold said, wishing he had not heard that last word, one he rarely if ever used and that was not appropriate for a professor. The ethos of the English department was to "keep it clean" at all times, out of respect for the students and also one's colleagues, to say nothing of the fine language they were responsible for teaching. "Like secondhand smoke," Dorothy would grumble when she heard a string of four-letter words, "sullies my air."

"Well, does it meet your standards now?" Frieda, dressed in the dark blazer and skirt that was her usual poetry-teaching uniform, stood in the doorway of the office with her hands on her hips. "Arn worked all Sunday on it."

"It's fine," Laurel said.

"Normally we don't do that sort of thing for a new hire," Frieda said. "No one cleaned my carpet for me, for example, when I came here. So I think it was above and beyond the call of duty for Arn to take the time." She checked her watch. "I'm off to class."

"Hey, Arn, thanks." Laurel's smile revealed gapless front teeth like perfect gleaming kernels of white corn. "It's not like I asked *you* to take care of the problem, as I recall. You said something about asking the dean to replace the carpet?"

"Ask I did, but as I suspected, the budget isn't generous enough for new carpets," Arnold said.

"Whatever. Well, thanks. I've got to get my butt in gear and unpack these books. Thank God I don't have to teach until tomorrow." Laurel gestured toward the boxes she had pushed into the office on a hand truck. "And where can I get an espresso around here?"

"The Java Moose is the campus coffeehouse. May I join you?" Arnold was startled to hear himself so boldly request her company, but it was not out of the range of acting-chair duties to buy a new hire a coffee.

"Got too much to do now, but maybe threeish?"

"That works," Arnold said, noting the casual tone of his response.

Gardenia held out a phone message as he passed her desk on the way to his office. "Your mother called."

"Thanks. I've asked her to leave messages on my cell, but she prefers to 'interact with a warm body,' as she would say."

At this Gardenia swiveled in her chair and opened the file drawer below the computer. I am quoting my mother, he thought, not trying to be suggestive by juxtaposing the words *interact*, *warm*, and *body*.

"Oh, it's no problem," Gardenia said. "She has a nice voice. I think what one would call dulcet."

"I'm sure she would consider it a compliment." Gardenia is the administrative assistant that the English department deserves, he thought as he offered Leroy a dog jerky stick and dug a cheese sandwich from his backpack for himself. *Dulcet*—Doris Breen had never used the word. The term did fit the sound of Dorothy Wiggens's voice, sweeter than one would expect for a woman who had edged past eighty years.

Arnold stepped into his office, closed the door, and pulled up the file on his laptop that contained the mass of words that was his manuscript. He had all day to work on his book, as his first class was scheduled for Tuesday. He soon became engrossed in smoothing out sentences and correcting typos, so much more soothing than cranking out original ideas that could hold the weight of yet-another academic's study of Chaucer. He ran spell check over the entire two hundred pages, briskly punching the Ignore command again and again as the program latched onto period names and places.

When Leroy began to murmur to go out for a bathroom break, Arnold saw that it was a quarter to three.

Time for the Java Moose. The door to Laurel's office was ajar, the light off. She had left without him.

She must have assumed that I meant to *meet* her at the Java Moose rather than walk over there together, Arnold thought. Now he had to give Leroy the time he needed on the campus lawns and also arrive at the Java Moose by threeish.

But Arnold could not resist examining Laurel's office for a few minutes first. The college-issued bookcases were neatly filled. On a small table near the window was an artful assemblage of shells and a tall green pottery vase, its curved neck bringing to mind that of a decapitated heron. A poster reproduction of a Picasso painting, with two children drawing on paper while their mother watched, leaned against the desk, ready to hang. In one corner was a jumble of empty boxes. Laurel must be accustomed to setting up a new office as she moved from one temporary appointment to another. Swiftly organizing one's office was one way to show professionalism and efficiency and thus "start the way you mean to go on," as his mother would say.

With Leroy on the leash, Arnold cut a path across the campus to the Java Moose. The balmy weather of the past week had turned to a gray chill, the bleak sky a disappointing contrast to the now gaudily blooming jonquil beds, the tulips about ready to burst open, and cherry blossoms in frothy array.

Laurel was not inside the coffee shop when he arrived. In one corner were two solid middle-aged women he knew from the library's front desk, about his age but as if of a completely different generation, with their fortified chins and complicated and dramatic family lives. A coed with tufts of short chartreuse hair sat at the counter, chatting up the young barista. Arnold tied Leroy to the leg of one of the outside tables, went inside, and ordered a cappuccino—he drank perhaps a half dozen espressos a year—and returned outside to sit with his dachshund.

He zipped his parka and toyed with the idea of pulling his hood up but decided that fickle Seattle spring weather or no, this was not the most attractive look to display to Laurel across the rickety metal bistro table. He wished he had brought the hand-knit muffler that his mother had given him the previous Christmas.

It was now past threeish, closer to three thirtyish. On a clean page of his little notebook, with the chunky pencil that desperately called for sharpening, he wrote: *Post-modern literature—what is its lineage?* Those who received doctorates in po-mo had to log a certain number of hours studying the literature that had come before, including Chaucer. I am genuinely curious to learn about how the classics reverberate in the moderns, he thought.

"Oh my God, I can't believe I walked to the end of the campus in the other direction, trying to find this place."

Laurel threw her arms out grandly as she said this, as if she expected to get a laugh. Arnold sprang to his feet, accidentally shoving Leroy with his left foot and causing the dog to yelp.

"Hey, no animal cruelty." She laughed, and Arnold joined in amiably, though he would never be cruel to Leroy, or any animal, for that matter.

"Please." He lifted his backpack from the other chair.

"Don't you want to go inside? It's freezing out here."

"Your choice."

Laurel's espresso of choice was not a macchiato but a nonfat mocha with, oddly, an extravagant cap of whipped cream. She took a swig.

"Jesus, you don't know how good it feels to have a job at a real university. I've done my bit, teaching all those crap community-college classes since I moved to the Northwest. And the dean said something about a tenure-track job. Wait—what's the deal with meetings around here?" Laurel wiped the rim of the cup with her index finger and licked off the traces of cream.

"We have them once a month," Arnold said.

"I can't stand sitting in meetings, listening to everyone trying to impress everyone else with their incredible research. And arguing over how many copies everyone gets to make every quarter. You should have heard them at West Cascade Community College, the discussions about whether office doors should be left open or closed."

"One might say we have an open-door policy about whether you open or close your door. Heh heh."

Laurel did not join his chuckle. "But if people want me to say something about my latest book, my PowerPoint show is fairly awesome, if I do say so myself." She pulled a ChapStick from the pocket of her red leather jacket and whisked it across her lips. "Yale published my dissertation and I started a new book while I was doing the freeway-flier adjunct gig. Who's your publisher?"

"Yale is interested." Arnold felt his face flush at this embellishment of the truth.

"Coincidence!"

Laurel wound her copious black-and-white scarf around her neck. The checkered pattern brought to mind images Arnold had seen of strident Middle Eastern protesters. Her gloves were of a soft leopard-patterned material, an exotic equatorial-zone contrast to her pale cold-country gestalt.

"Thanks for the mocha. My treat next time. Now I think I can find my way to my car. I've got to get home and review my lecture notes," she said.

"Starting a new position is one of the more preoccupying enterprises of human life," Arnold said but immediately regretted the sudden coagulation of his speech.

Laurel paused. "Yep, it's a bitch." Her delicate lips crooked into what many would call a smirk.

Back at his office, Arnold started in on his manuscript again. Yes, he would find a publisher for his book, and soon—if not Yale, another esteemed publishing house. He needed to show his scholarly vigor so that Dodge would stop subtly needling him. And when he and Laurel became better acquainted, he would share his manuscript and ask her to mention it to her editor at Yale. I hereby accept her prolificacy as a challenge and an inspiration, he thought.

By 10:00 p.m. Arnold had tapped out ten pages of a blowsy new chapter. An "SFD, Shitty First Draft" was what he had heard others call their initial pass on a piece of writing. Laurel would call it that, he thought.

Famished, Arnold carried Leroy the eight blocks to his apartment, wanting to arrive as quickly as possible to his supper of potato soup and a grilled chicken sausage. He wondered what sort of meal Laurel had fixed for herself that evening, or if she had stopped at one of the many small restaurants near campus. Thai food, perhaps. He had occasionally invited his colleagues to his apartment for a meal, confident in his ability to create a satisfying fish chowder and green salad and even a plum cake for dessert. Dorothy Wiggens had insisted that her son master "decent human being skills" while still in high school.

Why not invite Laurel over some evening? They could discuss their books, and he would tell her what he knew of the tenure process.

It had been a long time since a woman had piqued his curiosity. He would enjoy getting to know her as a colleague and settling into the comfortable rapport of two individuals who have dedicated themselves to purveying the delights of English literature, whether po-mo or Chaucerian.

Nothing wrong with that.

Chapter Six

"I PUBLISH ALL the time, so I hope you'll be able to help me get my manuscripts ready."

Laurel tossed a single-spaced manuscript and a thumb drive on Gardenia's desk.

"You'd be hard-pressed to find anyone who types as fast as I do," Gardenia bristled. It was perhaps not the greatest skill in the world, and not completely relevant in the computer age, but she had clacked away merrily on a Royal typewriter for eight weeks in junior-high summer school and since then had usually tested at more than ninety words a minute.

"It's not typing. I need you to reformat this, spell-check it, and all that. By three thirty. I told the editor I'd submit it by email attachment by the end of the day. OK with that?"

"No worries." Gardenia regretted the chipper sound of her own voice.

"Well, cool." Laurel chucked her junk mail in the recycling bin and swayed in her platform sandals down the hall to her office. Gardenia wondered what happened to the male students when Dr. DuBarr appeared at the lectern. Someone's research had shown that college students think about sex about ninety percent of their waking hours. Professors ought to work a little harder at being dowdy, Gardenia thought. Laurel could take Frieda Hamm as an example and wear soft flat shoes and a frumpy black skirt, hair cut short and glasses with outdated frames.

"Your first project from Dr. DuBarr." Arnold peered at the manuscript where it rested on an upright clipboard by Gardenia's computer and read a sentence aloud: "*The oeuvre of Thomas Pynchon offers a plethora of interpretations, not the least of which is based on adopting the premises of psychoanalysis and applying these to the author's choices in developing interhuman dynamics and finding echoes for these in the specifics of setting and atmosphere.*" He sighed. "Ah."

Gardenia waited for Arnold to chuckle or lift his eyebrows in a "What in the world does she mean?" expression, but instead he said, "We're lucky to have Dr. DuBarr."

"She wants me to reformat and spell-check it by three thirty. I should be able to finish if I don't get interrupted by students." Gardenia's first week on the job had been filled with what would be an English department definition of *mayhem*. Students slouched in and out with various official forms, anxious—some in tears—about their class schedules and graduation requirements.

As if on cue, a coed slumped by Gardenia's desk and moaned, "It's going to be a disaster if I don't get out of this philosophy class and into something else. I couldn't understand a word the prof was saying. Don't you have a good English class that I could take?'

"Ah, the eternal myth of the easy grade from the English department," said Arnold. "Maybe you would like to try an introduction to one of the finest raconteurs of the English language?"

"Uh, OK?"

"I suggest Introduction to Geoffrey Chaucer and His World. It's been in the top ten of the department evaluations," Arnold said.

"Whatever. Nothing about philosophy, right?"

"Not even a suggestion."

Gardenia checked and noted that the enrollment was still half open.

The girl, now duly transferred, put two thumbs up to show her satisfaction before nearly skipping out of the office in her fleece boots.

"Pardon my salesmanship," Arnold said, "but as Dodge is so willing to remind us, we in the liberal arts have to woo the Youth of Today away from computer science and business."

"I remember that the English classes, the ones where you actually read books, were always my favorite," Gardenia said. "Though I had a hard time writing papers. Wasn't it enough just to like the book?"

"Indeed. But we justify our salaries by toiling through undergraduate papers."

Gardenia handed Laurel the formatted and freshly printed manuscript just before three thirty.

"Thanks, appreciated," Laurel said, glancing up for only a split second from her cell phone.

We old birds aren't as useless as we look, Gardenia almost said. Next time I'm not going to sit here like a misused valet, she thought. I'm going to tell her to put down her phone when she speaks to me.

But no, I won't. Administrative assistants don't speak in cheeky tones to PhD professors. And I need this job.

Oh, Torre, if only we had imagined my being a widow and made sure there was enough money! she wanted to shout. *It's your fault I ran out of money and have to work this demeaning job!*

Well, that wasn't true. They had both earned a little less than they should have, saved less, known less about investing. And she had used a big chunk of her modest life-insurance payout to replace an aged sewer line and a leaking roof and the transmission in her old Subaru.

Arnold, carrying a white paper bag and with Leroy trotting beside him on the leash, joined Gardenia in the elevator at the end of the day.

"All is well?" he asked.

"I finished Dr. DuBarr's project," Gardenia said, "but I wonder if she's even going to look at it before she emails it tonight." Realizing she sounded annoyed, Gardenia wished she had kept her mouth shut. She was not only griping about the work she was asked to do but also making a critical remark about Arnold's colleague. "I mean, at least she had it by the time she wanted."

"Anything we can do to help her with her publishing also makes the department look good."

Barely knowing Arnold, Gardenia could not be expected to read his face fluently, but his animation as he spoke even a few sentences about the glamorous young professor proved another aphorism from the dry cleaners: *Two things one cannot hide on the face—a toothache and being in love.*

Arnold extended the paper bag with its logo of a nearby Italian restaurant. "They made a mistake on my order, so they offered me an extra panini, free of charge. Please."

And they say there is no such thing as a free lunch, Gardenia thought as she politely demurred twice before accepting the bag. A sandwich offered out of the blue by anyone else, and I'd feel that I now was obligated in some way to the other person, but I doubt it would ever occur to the guileless Arnold to expect something in return.

If only he didn't have to veer into that stilted way of speaking, sounding as if he just strolled in from the nineteenth century. But if his filigreed speech managed to keep Dr. Laurel DuBarr at arm's length, all the better. She wasn't good enough for him, her selfishness already evident. Arnold Wiggens deserves a kind, smart woman, Gardenia thought.

Just as Hans deserves.

And just as Caitlin is *not*.

AT HOME AT her kitchen table, with the panini and a chubby juice glass filled with pinot grigio, Gardenia studied a flyer that a male student had handed her on the way to the parking garage: *Free! 7:30 p.m. World Percussion Ensemble. Get the Rhythm, Get the Beat!* A note at the bottom of the page explained that the concert had been cancelled winter quarter because of a water leak in the theater and so was rescheduled for that evening, the start of spring quarter.

Gardenia ate half the panini and carefully decanted the wine back into its budget-priced jug. Well, why not venture out? Why spend another night by herself in front of the TV? She would enjoy telling Hans that she had been *out*, doing something cultural and perhaps even vaguely hip.

By seven fifteen she had settled in a seat near the middle of the auditorium. The percussionists plodded about the stage, arranging their considerable arsenal of drums, marimbas, rhythm blocks, and shakers. On the program was the name of a boy who lived a few blocks away and had gone to elementary school with Hans. In the front row sat his now-gray-haired mother, Marian, looking much older than Gardenia remembered.

I hope I don't run into Marian after the concert, Gardenia thought. It's been years since I've spoken with her, and I don't want to endure that uncomfortable moment of Comparing How Old We Look. And I'm not up for any hen-clucking about "How are you doing, you must be so lonely?" or its equally unwelcome counterpart, cheery conversation that completely avoids the subject of dead Torre. Gardenia decided to stay in her seat during the intermission and, when the concert was over, leave the auditorium well after Marian had departed.

Across the aisle sat a dark-haired phalanx of Asian students, their pens poised to take notes. An ESL class, perhaps, assigned to see a multicultural event. From far-off lands, their mothers—waiting anxiously for emails or phone calls—sent packages with aromatic sauces and dried fish or whatever else would bear the flavor of home, even though few undergrads were likely to cook. Besides, the main drag near campus was festooned with small soy-sauce-fragrant eateries offering cheap Chinese and Thai and Vietnamese food. And the inevitable slabs of teriyaki chicken, though she had read that this was a Seattle invention and nowhere to be found in Japan.

At least their mothers don't have to worry about a daughter-in-law who may have a lover, Gardenia thought. In Asian countries, wasn't it the young husbands who had girlfriends or even liaisons with prostitutes? Or was this a myth, left over from a previous age, before young women left their countries to be educated in foreign lands, only to return with enlightened feminist principles to apply to their own lives?

The performance started with a half dozen male students—their wrinkled black shirts and slacks revealing their distance from the maternal ironing board—who struck the marimba and timpani and snare drums. How remarkable that the world had a way to envelop young people with percussion training! Well, you might as well bang on drums or shake ethnic rattles while you're an undergrad, Gardenia thought, because eventually your days start to close in, other far less lively choices hectoring for your attention.

"Gardenia," came a deep whisper from two rows behind her.

It was that man Lex, who had shared her table at Café Venezia.

The fingers of her right hand flittered in a wave, and she was glad that the theater was dark, the better to hide her blush. What a strange coincidence to see this man again, so soon after first speaking to him. She'd googled him and learned that Lex Ohashi was a structural engineer and had served on the Seattle Japanese Garden advisory board. He did not have a Facebook page. No other names were listed with his in the online white pages.

Her concentration drifted from the enthusiastic thumping and banging of instruments as she rehearsed what she would say to him.

When the house lights went up at intermission, Lex slipped into the seat beside her.

"I never imagined I would see you here," he said.

"Do you know one of the musicians?" Gardenia replied with what she hoped was the neutral tone appropriate for conversation with an almost stranger.

"Yep. My niece plays the marimba. Her parents are in Idaho. So I try to stay on her radar. I enjoy it." He folded his muffler as if he meant to add it to a haberdasher's display case. "And who do you know?"

"No one. Well, Austin, who grew up down the street from us, but I haven't seen him in years. I saw the flyer and thought the concert sounded interesting."

What to do, what to do? I know nothing about this man, Gardenia thought, except that he drinks straight espresso and likes lemon tarts and is adept at folding mufflers. That his real name is Lester but he's called Lex. And that he is attractive in a dark-eyed, chipped-tooth, silver-templed way.

She had blurted out to Lex that her husband was dead, so maybe he imagined she was vulnerable and *easy prey*. She'd feel better if at least she knew whether he was married—no wedding ring, but nowadays people had partners or even spouses but no adornment to indicate this.

"It must mean a lot to her, to have an aunt and uncle nearby," Gardenia said, surprised by her shrewdness in finding out what she needed to know without asking directly.

"*Aunt?* Oh, you mean my wife? Don't have one of those. Amanda just has a doting uncle."

The house lights went down. Lex draped his taut left forearm on the armrest between them, a simple gesture that was bold and proprietary. Usually with strangers, you do not colonize the armrest at all, to make sure you are not overstepping a territorial boundary. His blue chambray shirt was rolled up to show a manly crop of dark hair on the back of his arms, and his jaw was outlined with what used to be called a five o'clock shadow. No one called it that anymore, as a scruffy, unshaven look seemed to be the fashion.

As he leaned half a degree into the airspace surrounding her seat, Gardenia caught the aroma of coffee that he had apparently just drunk, a whiff of underarm perspiration, and the clean fragrance of some sort of soap, maybe the kind dispensed in the auditorium restroom.

She had spoken with this man Lex only once before. She was fifty-six years old, long married and out of circulation, and yet she recognized a surge of feeling that she had experienced at other moments in her life: sitting behind a redheaded boy with long dark eyelashes on the first day of kindergarten; holding hands as the folk-dancing partner of a fifth-grade boy with a gorgeous smile; walking onto the gym floor to dance with a lanky basketball player at the seventh-grade mixer. In high school and college, she had had regular crushes. Only with Torre had there not been that heated rush of sexual attraction that made her feel like a scarlet poppy in full slatternly bloom.

Later she understood that the easy comfort she immediately felt with him was true love.

The musicians added a row of steel and African drums of various sizes. As they began to beat out a rhythm, one of the young men chanted, a titch off-key, some words in a foreign language that two other students called back to him. The African creators of this music would have held their sides while bursting with laughter at the sight of the sedate audience, listening to the enticing beats as if to a Wagner opera, Gardenia thought. Well, maybe those in the audience would have been less stodgy if the musicians had been shirtless, showing strongly muscled chests and perhaps wearing sarongs with flamboyant designs instead of shirts and pants that clearly had been rescued at the last minute from the overloaded laundry basket.

"Why aren't we dancing to this?" Lex whispered.

Gardenia pulled a pen from the pocket of her parka and scribbled on the program: *It's as if some other culture learned how to make ornate Western pastries but put them out for show, not for anyone to eat.*

Lex took the pen and wrote: *LOL.*

As if he had read Gardenia's mind, the instructor said when the piece was finished, "I'm sure you know that drumming in many cultures is always the signal for dancing. So we invite you to join us on the stage and rock out."

A half dozen students began to gyrate to the fresh round of percussion, with some of the black-clad performers from the first set starting a conga line, like young priests called in to help with the youth program sock hop.

"Come on!" Lex grabbed Gardenia's hand as he stood up.

"Oh, I don't know, in front of all these people . . ."

"The pastries are meant to be eaten, not just looked at," he whispered.

So she found herself being led to the stage by this fragrant man she barely knew, his hand warm and firm as it wrapped around hers. As Lex clasped her waist in the conga line, she wondered if he detected the soft pads of flesh on her upper hips. At least she had a waist to hold on to, unlike some women her age whose bodies perfectly suited the term *trunk*, as broad and undefined as an aged cedar.

The next piece caused the other dancers to snake their arms in the air—much as Gardenia remembered dancing as a college student—but Lex pulled her into ballroom mode and led her in a two-step that followed the beat.

At least no one I know is watching, ready to gossip about me and the new man in my life, she thought. But wait. Marian, in the front row. Maybe she won't recognize me, as I almost didn't recognize her.

Gardenia held herself as far away from Lex as the mechanics of dancing allowed, a warning voice clicking on in her head. Careful, careful with men when you first meet them. Charmers are often the ones who pan out the worst. They snare you and play around with you while you're in the net and walk away when they're tired of you. Or so it seemed from novels and movies and BBC series about romance. But she relaxed as she fell into step with Lex, a sure-footed dancer. I do love to dance, she thought, and it's been so long—the last time had been years ago, at a friend's wedding, when she had convinced the reluctant Torre that it would be impolite not to join the other guests on the dance floor.

When the piece ended one of the black-clads dashed behind the baffle at the back of the stage and emerged with a long white pole.

"Limbo!" he shouted.

"I'm going to give it a shot while the pole is pretty high," Lex said. "Come on!"

And so Gardenia found herself awkwardly hopping under the limbo pole, Lex following after her but straining more than she did because of his height. The second time she went under the now-lowered pole, she bent back as far as she thought she could possibly go and made it under. Lex, spreading his feet apart and making short jumps as the nimble students had done, nonetheless fell with a thwack on his behind.

In a split second Gardenia considered her choices: If I rush in to help him, will I offend his manhood? If I don't rush in to help him, am I being inconsiderate? Maybe he hurt himself. Should I yell out to call 911? Or should I pretend I was looking the other way and didn't see it happen?

Lex stood up quickly, took an exaggerated bow to the others, and brushed off the back of his jeans.

"I'm done," he said, "but you can try again."

"You're OK?" Gardenia ventured, hoping that he heard this as simply one human's concern for another when a limbo execution ends in a sudden plop onto the hard floor.

"I'm fine."

"These students are too lively for my speed." Which they were, but she also wanted to give both of them an excuse to opt out of any other challenging Caribbean dance.

The niece, who was now taking her turn holding the limbo pole, waved at Uncle Lex.

Lex gently coaxed Gardenia with the hand-on-the-back maneuver to their seats.

When the concert ended, she extended her hand. "Thanks for getting me up there to dance."

"My pleasure indeed. I've always liked to dance, but it's not that easy to find a good partner," he said.

"Really? I thought dance floors were lined with women who need partners."

He smiled, showing the chipped tooth. "My mother always told me I had to ask at least two girls to dance besides the one I took as a date. Which I almost never did."

"That weird high school culture. You were supposed to stick with one guy all night long. I don't think they do that anymore. My son and his friends went in a big group to prom, nobody had a date."

"My niece did that. And seems like the big deal was to rent a hotel room after the dance and hang out all night. My sister had a fit and wouldn't let her. I guess Amanda survived as the only uncool girl in the world."

"Our son insisted on the hotel after-party. Torre said I needed to trust my own kid, so I gave in. But I've never felt good about it."

Lex's phone pinged. When he pulled it from his blazer pocket and turned away slightly to check the text, Gardenia said nothing even though she thought this rude. But maybe it was best to have broken the thread about hotel rooms.

"How can I get in touch with you again?" He held his phone expectantly, waiting for her to give him her number.

"You can email me at the English department at UNW," she said. "I open all the English department emails."

"Let's go dancing sometime. Maybe the Cascade Ballroom?"

"Sure," she was surprised to hear herself say.

In the dim glow from the streetlights in the parking lot, her face in the Subaru's rear-view mirror looked slimmer than she recalled. I am still presentable, Gardenia thought. Her hair was a deep brown, and her olive-toned complexion protected her from the wrinkles that fair-skinned women—Dr. Laurel DuBarr, for example—showed at a young age.

Gardenia tossed and turned that night, unable to get to sleep until after two in the morning, missing Torre all the more as she wondered about this man who had suddenly appeared in her life and seemed interested in courting her.

Chapter Seven

No instructor at the University of the Northwest could possibly look forward to teaching a class as much as I look forward to this session of Introduction to Geoffrey Chaucer and His World, Arnold thought as he stood in front of his ten students, the patches of April sunshine from the south-facing classroom window like cheerful spotlights on the worn wooden floorboards.

But I don't look forward to what I have to say to begin the session. Clearing his throat, he addressed the group.

"Ladies and gentlemen, today we'll access the brilliance of Mr. Geoffrey Chaucer in a way that would bring him sheer delight. It may even bring some of *you* sheer delight. I'm certain that it will offer me sheer delight. But first, I request that you put all cell phones and laptops and any other device that has you in its electronic snare on the table by the door."

The students glared at him as if they had been asked to remove their clothes.

"Back in the day, as the saying goes, students sat and listened to the professor and took notes on paper with a pen or pencil. The teacher himself would have managed with a mere blackboard and piece of chalk."

All but one of the students dutifully set their laptops and cell phones on the table.

"We can't even keep our phones? My mom was going to text me," said the young woman who had enrolled in his class to avoid the tortures of philosophy. Was she Taylor, or Mackenzie, or Madison? With only ten names to remember, he should have known who this girl was, but he was flummoxed by the many given names that had once been only surnames.

Fortunately *Wiggens* was not included in this trend.

"Your mother wouldn't want to interrupt," Arnold said, controlling himself so that he didn't add: "And why would she want to distract you from a class that she is paying such a high price for you to take?"

"Whatever." Taylor-Mackenzie-Madison arranged her laptop and cell next to the others on the table.

"So what do we do now?" asked another girl—Arnold thought her name was Courtney but he'd have to check the class list. She slumped in her desk, arms crossed and slender legs stretched in front of her as if to more adequately display her purple flip-flops and matching painted toenails.

"Please find a partner and open your copy of *The Tales* to page two. I'd like you to take turns reading the first eighteen lines of the prologue to each other, then skip ahead to page one hundred eighty-two and start reading the tale of the Wife of Bath aloud. Though at a low volume."

"The English part, right?" said Ms. Flip-Flops, who seemed to be the ad hoc spokesperson for the group. "No way I could pronounce the old English stuff."

"I want you to read the *original* to each other. The listener should not refer to the text. There's no better way to understand the genius of Mr. Chaucer than to recite his perfectly rhymed couplets as they were written."

If rolled eyes could make a sound, Arnold thought, this room would rumble with disgruntlement. But the students found partners, shoved their desks together, and began reading.

Arnold knew how this class session would proceed. First, the cautious reading of the first lines—did they notice the seasonal appropriateness of *Aprill*? Next, the conferring about how to pronounce the *e*'s at the end of words. (He had explained Middle English pronunciation in the third class session, and eventually some students would remember.)

The chuckling and "Oh my God"-ing as they fumbled to intone the lines. Inevitably one student (it turned out, interestingly, to be Ms. Flip-Flops) would cover up the awkwardness by adding dramatic flourishes. And after about fifteen minutes, each pair would settle into a kind of flow and satisfaction as they realized that they *could* understand the recited lines, even without seeing them on the page.

He chose to focus on the Wife of Bath because her saucy tale was a sure crowd-pleaser. What undergrad would not be interested in reading about that lusty old gal, who declared that human bodies were made as much for pleasure as for function, and shouldn't they be enjoyed accordingly?

Coincidentally two of the student pairs were tracking almost exactly so that the readers recited in unison: "*I pray you, telleth me; / Or wher comanded he virginitee?*"

Laughter.

"And what is going on here?

Hamilton Dodge stood in the doorway.

"Ah, Dean Dodge." Arnold raised his hand in a salute of greeting.

"I was passing and heard all the racket. I thought maybe a bunch of students were hanging out without permission."

"Several times a quarter I ask the students to take turns reading to each other from the original text," Arnold said. "The best way to appreciate Chaucer." And it is perfectly defensible pedagogical technique, Arnold wanted to add, one that the students always say they appreciate.

"*I pray you, telleth me; / Or wher comanded he virginitee?*" Ms. Flip-Flops reprised. "It's kind of cool once you get into it."

If I had less integrity, Arnold thought, I would add ten gratis points to Ms. Flip-Flop's next essay exam in thanks for this remark.

Who was Dodge to barge in on his class, anyway?

At that moment a reciter, undeterred by Dodge's appearance, intoned: "*Virginitee is greet perfeccioun*" which caused more laughter.

Dodge shook his head, muttered "Oh, *Wiggens*," and tramped from the room.

The students recited without complaint until the class ended, a vindication of the recitation exercise as well as the validity of teaching Mr. Chaucer's work in the first place. With any luck all these students will enroll in my Middle English class in the fall, Arnold thought.

"Hey, that was actually pretty awesome," Taylor-Mackenzie-Madison said. "I mean, it was cool the way you could actually understand most of it, without looking at the real English part."

"I didn't mind just using a book either," one of the young men said. "A change from everything on a screen."

"Mr. Chaucer wrote with a quill pen dipped in ink on coarse expensive paper. Even fountain pens were centuries away," Arnold said.

But no one responded to this, as the students were collecting their laptops and phones and heading out the door.

When Arnold returned to the English department offices, Dodge was chatting with Gardenia.

"An interesting glimpse into your teaching methods," he said. "Who knew that reading aloud would keep them engaged like that?"

"My teachers in grade school read aloud to us after lunch," Gardenia said as she picked up a stack of mail to distribute. "It was always my favorite part of school."

Well, Dodge's sudden appearance was not as ominous as it had seemed. His comments could be interpreted as neutral to slightly positive, Arnold thought.

Back in his office he snapped on Leroy's leash to take him outside for a walk in the *April* noontide. The last cherry blossoms had sifted over the campus lawns, and tulips were claiming the bed where he had plucked a jonquil. No springtime could be more beautiful than that of Seattle, he thought, though "olde England" must have been similar, with its damp moderate climate.

Warm days were still a long way off, the spring coming on slowly with the first camellia blooms in late February but shifting between fiftyish-degree days to those in the upper sixties until nearly the end of June, with stretches of clouds and rain and only a day here and there that spiked above seventy.

Spring weather or no, he would use the afternoon to work on his manuscript. Who knew? Perhaps with an introduction to Laurel's editor, a publishing contract would be a slam dunk.

The next morning an email from Dodge popped up, saying he wanted to meet with Arnold within the week to discuss an important matter.

Chapter Eight

THE MEMO FROM Human Resources had explained that employees were to submit time cards by the twentieth of each month, with paychecks issued on the tenth of the next month. Any hours not reported by the twentieth would be added to the accounting for the subsequent paycheck. The welcome words *paycheck* and *payroll* tucked into the text had diverted Gardenia from understanding that since she officially was hired after March 20, she would not receive a paycheck until May 10.

In her bank account was exactly $2,296.23. Thirteen hundred of this was needed for the mortgage and eighty for car insurance and a couple hundred more for various bills. This left all of about $700 for gas and food to last nearly two months.

In the pantry were a box of whole wheat rotini, a can of water chestnuts, a bag of quinoa, three cans of black beans, sugar, flour, oil, and a bottle of maple syrup. The freezer held some frozen vegetables, orange juice, and a box of Danish pastries. At least I can "whip up a batch of pancakes," Gardenia thought, the hearty tone of this phrase belying how she felt about having to figure out how to keep herself going until she received her first check.

She would pack a lunch and even a thermos of coffee, and she could make some soup and a pasta casserole and get cheap bananas and apples at the discount Lucky Produce Market, that last resting place of less-than-perfect grocery store produce.

Collecting a canvas grocery bag from the jumble of old hats and scarves in the basket in the front closet, Gardenia set off for Lucky Produce, on a corner a few blocks from where Hans had gone to high school. Seattle was always ripe, as it were, with young people willing to work the cash register and stack piles of celery and misshapen yams and about-to-rot bananas and pears. The female cashiers had moved from the era of long hippie hair and no bras into dreadlocks and nose and lip piercings and tattoos. Some of the young men had shaved heads nowadays rather than cascading Jesus locks, but they seemed to Gardenia to be descendants of the earlier tribe.

At least my Hans is an employee of a legitimate natural foods store with four walls and a professionally designed logo and a newsletter and insurance benefits, Gardenia thought. She couldn't bear to think of her son working at Lucky Produce, his hands in fingerless gloves in the middle of winter, the chilly sodden air blasting into the wall-less fourth side of the store.

A clerk, looking with his septum ring like a cherubic blue-eyed bullock, was picking through a pile of Fuji apples, tossing the culls into a cardboard box layered with shaggy lettuce leaves.

"What do you do with the apples you put in the box?" Gardenia asked.

"Dumpster. At a certain point even we can't sell end-of-the-line stuff." He held up an apple with a ragged brown bruise.

"If I find an apple like that in my fridge, I cut off the bad spot and eat the rest."

The young man smiled stiffly, showing what looked to be the handiwork of a skilled orthodontist. Gardenia imagined him regaling his roommates, while they passed a joint around their rickety dining room table, with tales of an old biddy who dithered about apple bruises, but he said, "I do too."

"Do they let you take these home?"

He leaned toward her conspiratorially. "Yes and no. Officially we can't because if we got sick from eating something bad, we could sue the boss. Blah blah. But I take home boxes for me and my housemates. I put the rest in the garbage. I have two boxes in the back that are heading there."

"I'll take them," Gardenia squeaked.

"Can't do that," he said loudly, pulling two more apples out of the pile, but he winked at her and motioned with his head toward the back of the store. "Meet me by the Dumpster."

Before sneaking behind the store, Gardenia spent $3.53 on four carrots, a half dozen large dusty beets, and a giant yam that would have done fine in the ring with a spaghetti squash.

"Gardenia?"

This voice she had not heard for years, not since Hans had graduated from high school, but Gardenia recognized immediately the shrill tone of Mary Newsome-Jones. Her son, Jacob, had been the other accomplished pianist in the high school jazz band.

Juilliard had given him a full ride.

"Hi, Mary." Gardenia waved from where she stood by the Dumpster.

"I haven't seen you since the boys graduated!" Mary said. "I'm on my way to help with the high school jazz band auction. They need us, you know, even when our own kids aren't part of the band anymore."

Oh, the cloying way that Mary would always list, with a tidy smile of false humility, the good works that she had done—for the jazz band or some group of needy or disabled children or a one-legged athlete running a marathon! Gardenia remembered the sideways remarks comparing their two boys: "Jacob practices at least four hours a day. He gets up before we do and we hear him at it. But it paid off, that's why he got into so many schools."

"Anyway, it's been *ages!*" Mary called. "How is Hans doing? Jacob is done at Juilliard, and he's doing a master's."

"Good for him," Gardenia said.

"I don't shop here, I have to say. I saw a roach once, on the zucchini. Disgusting! But I'd love to hear your news. I haven't heard Jacob mention Hans since they graduated."

The young produce worker appeared with a battered box full of tired lettuce, compromised oranges, and pears. "Here you go. Not too heavy. I'll get the other one."

"Oh, *Gardenia*." Mary's tone was pitying, accusatory, scolding, or all three.

"I'm taking these to the homeless shelter," Gardenia snapped as she accepted the box. She felt a shimmer of tears but managed to say, "I can't stand to see food wasted. Some of it is perfectly good."

Mary wrinkled her nose. "That stuff smells like it's going bad, for sure. I hope the homeless don't get sick or anything. You can always dump it into the yard-waste bin. Anyway, it was great to see you! We should have coffee sometime!"

Mary, responding to a text on her phone, waved like a celebrity on a parade float and strode toward the high school.

"Thanks," Gardenia said to the produce worker when he returned with the second box. "I hope you don't get in trouble."

"Naw, the boss doesn't mind. Hang on just a minute."

He ducked into the back and returned with a jumbo bag of tortilla chips.

"Past the pull date. My roomies are getting sick of tortilla chips. Hey, you can have a par-tay!"

Gardenia wanted to hug him or ask for his mother's phone number so she could compliment her on the matter-of-fact thoughtfulness of this young man.

"I'm Gardenia, by the way." She extended her hand.

"Christopher." He held up his grimy palms to explain why he wasn't going to shake.

"Thanks, Christopher. I shop here a lot, so I hope I see you again."

"No worries."

Touched by Christopher's kindness, Gardenia decided she wouldn't care about the annoying Mary Newsome-Joneses of the world. I never liked her much anyway, she thought. And the other kids in the band had smelled the stink of competition on Jacob. This wasn't a problem when the band was working together to win some competition but a turnoff when he jockeyed for more solos or made a big deal about winning an outstanding musician award.

No way was she going to mention Jacob's master's degree to Hans, but Gardenia felt tears in her eyes again. She wished her boy could be strolling through the busy streets of the Upper West Side after a day pounding away on the piano and receiving expert instruction from some of the world's greatest musicians.

Chapter Nine

Arnold had no idea why the dean needed to see him.

Dodge left a message with Gardenia that he had a bad cold, so he wanted Arnold to meet him at his home in the Montlake neighborhood. The afternoon was clear, and Arnold decided he would walk rather than drive or take the bus. He delivered Leroy to his apartment and set out.

A gathering several years before at the dean's Craftsman bungalow near the arboretum had started with warm September weather but midway, a cold rain fell, forcing the guests to cluster in the kitchen, dining room, and living room and causing the first Mrs. Dodge much consternation. She kept repeating how lovely it was to be on the deck at that time of year. Arnold had reassured her at the end of the evening that the inside of their home had "perfectly suited a large gathering." This was the sort of thing Dorothy would have said, and although he meant it sincerely, he was half annoyed at his pearly good manners.

But Dodge's house was shabbier than he recalled, the planter boxes on the porch cradling only dirt and dried leaves despite the salubrious conditions for planting early annuals. The gray porch paint was peeling. A faded *Obama 2008* poster was propped under one of the front windows.

Angelina, the second Mrs. Dodge, answered the doorbell.

"Professor Wiggens, come in. My husband is expecting you. He's been coughing all night."

"I am sorry to hear that." Perhaps the dean was contagious. Whatever this meeting was about, it had better be worth the risk of catching a cold, Arnold thought.

"He's sitting in there. May I take your jacket?" Angelina, illuminated in the wan sunlight seeping into the foyer from the slender windows that flanked the door, was older than in the photo on Dodge's desk. Silver strands threaded through her dark hair, and creases framed her mouth and eyes when she smiled. She could be in her late forties or even early fifties, Arnold thought, which makes her closer to Dodge's age than I had imagined.

"Ah, there he is," Dodge rasped from where he sat on a tall-backed Mission-style armchair, his lap covered with a plaid blanket. "The wife insisted that I not leave the house today."

"I tell him that pneumonia happens all the time in old guys." Angelina collected some wadded-up tissues and rapped her husband's hunched back. "He can stay home and take care for a few days."

"Safe rather than sorry," Arnold suggested.

"Oh, she's a fusser," Dodge said when Angelina had left to fetch some tea. "Comes from all those years as a nurse, I guess. But nothing wrong with someone taking care of you as the years start to pile up, eh, Wiggens?"

"Ah" was all Arnold could manage, as he had no "fusser" in his life, if one did not count his mother, who *was* prone to worrying about him. He did not see her or speak to her every day, though, so he could contract a cold or the flu and be completely cured before she even knew.

Angelina handed each of them a Seattle tourist mug, Dodge's with a design of the Space Needle and Arnold's with the Mariners logo.

"Green tea, better for vitamins," she explained. "He prefers coffee, but I say no, only green tea when you are sick."

Dodge smiled meekly as he accepted the mug.

The doorbell rang.

"Oh, my niece," Angelina said. "Excuse me now, she's bringing her children, so we will stay in the kitchen to not bother you."

"Big on family, she is," Dodge said. "Angelina is the favorite aunt and all that. Usually they make the children shake hands with all the adults, but she said she didn't want them to get germs, so we won't see them."

The clamor of children's voices and the chattering of the aunt and niece seeped from the entry hall.

"I thought with my two grown, I was done with kids. And the mess." Dodge waved at the bins of Legos in one corner of the room and what seemed to be dress-up tutus and superhero costumes. Four Barbie dolls lay in a heap by the fireplace, one completely naked, like sad victims of a natural disaster. "But we're not talking about family life now, are we, Arn?"

"Not my topic of expertise," Arnold said.

"Your expertise, yes. That's why we need to talk." Dodge leaned forward and turned his head, aiming what must have been his better ear toward Arnold. "What can you tell me about that, old man?"

"*Tell* you?"

"About your book and publishing and so on."

"Yale has the full manuscript under consideration." Arnold hoped he would not have to reveal that "under consideration" meant only acknowledgment of receipt of his query and sample chapters.

"The way it stands now, the horse is out of the barn."

"I beg your pardon?"

"Water under the bridge, milk already spilled, cat's out of the bag." Dodge swigged his green tea. "I think you can guess what I'm getting at here."

Arnold felt his face grow warm. Whatever Dodge intended by this clumsy collation of sayings, it did not seem to be in the good news category.

"I'll be blunt. It's already been decided. No more college funds wasted on Chaucer. You know as well as I do that you barely fill ten chairs in your classroom. Time to move on. Gludger's position too. Need the funds to hire another tenure-track candidate in the modern stuff."

"Chaucer has always been an essential part of an English degree." Arnold said.

"*An essential part of an English degree*," Dodge said, his sketchy hearing perhaps blotting out the "Chaucer" part of Arnold's response. "English comp *is* the essential part of the English degree. Starting in the fall you'll teach three sections of freshman comp. Chaucer is off the menu. What use do these young ones have for a story about a bunch of people in merry olde England?" He pronounced the *e* at the end of *olde* and chuckled.

Fortunately Dodge descended into a coughing spasm that lasted long enough for Arnold to compose himself, as it were, and not respond immediately to this news. Angelina bustled in from the kitchen with water in a large purple plastic tumbler of the type used for beer at tailgate parties.

"I tell you, tomorrow you see the doctor if you don't stop coughing."

"It does sound as if you don't feel well at all." Arnold stood up and handed her his half-full mug.

"You don't like green tea?"

"It is tasty, but I must be on my way. Thank you for your hospitality."

"I can get your jacket," she said. Arnold wished he had not surrendered it to her when he arrived so he could manage a quicker getaway.

Dodge blew his nose on a fresh tissue.

"Sure you don't want to discuss this some more?"

"Seems there is nothing to discuss, the horse having departed the barn and the cat, the bag," Arnold said crisply but softly, wagering that his words would not be audible. "I assume others in the department know of this change in my status?"

"Of course not." Dodge might not have been so deaf after all. "I needed to discuss it with you first. I'll be bringing it up at the department meeting. I'm sure you won't take this personally, old chap. Teaching comp isn't the end of the world. And who knows? Maybe you can find a way to make them write a halfway literate term paper."

Inserting small bamboo skewers beneath my fingernails would be preferable to spending my working life reading crabbed freshman prose, Arnold thought, but he said only, "Indeed. I hope you feel better soon."

He accepted his jacket from Angelina and stepped out into gentle spring air, his throat aching with the need to shriek, either in rage or humiliation or both.

Chapter Ten

THE UNIVERSITY OF the Northwest slipped some half-day Fridays into each term, the first scheduled for the second week of April. Frieda Hamm had eagerly insisted that Gardenia visit her for tea on this free afternoon.

"I'd like to show you my teacup collection," she'd said.

Gardenia would have preferred to stay home and take Susie for some walks and tidy up the yard, but she had accepted the invitation, thinking it would be prudent not to offend anyone in the department. It would be interesting to find out more about Frieda's obvious crush on Arnold Wiggens, if this information was to be had over a cuppa.

Frieda's apartment was a few blocks from UNW, in one of the older brick buildings near a large hospital and medical clinics. Gardenia wondered if, back in the day, some developer had created these three- to four-story apartment buildings for the nurses who worked in the hospitals. "Career girls"—nurses or secretaries or teachers—used to live their whole lives in apartments. As single women they had no customary right to aspire to owning a tidy little home among married people with children.

Because the apartments were near the crest of First Hill, from the upper floors these hardworking women might have had a view of ferryboats chugging across the Sound; on a fine day they may have started their mornings with a view of the tips of the Olympics beyond Bainbridge Island. But that was before the neighborhood and downtown Seattle had filled with skyscrapers. No way Frieda had any view now.

Frieda buzzed Gardenia into the large foyer, complete with an arched entryway and small decorative stained-glass windows. The women who dwelt here for thirty or forty years must have kept themselves nimble and trim with all the climbing of the wide central staircase, Gardenia thought.

"You found me," Frieda said as she opened the door. "Shoes off, please. You can put them under that bench."

Gardenia did as she was told and discovered immediately that her thin socks were no match for the slick, cold oak floors, with only a small wool rug under the coffee table. Frieda had the benefit of a pair of large leather slippers.

"I hope you aren't gluten intolerant. Or lactose intolerant, for that matter," Frieda said as she plopped a plate of scones on the coffee table.

"I eat everything. Those look wonderful."

"My signature recipe. The key is oatmeal added to the flour. And real butter. Do you want some jam?" Frieda asked.

"If it's no trouble." *A clumsy hostess,* Gardenia thought, *which somehow I expected from Frieda—one is supposed to imagine that a guest wants jam and have it ready on the tea tray, particularly when this is her first visit to your home, and her feet are freezing.*

"I'm making PG Tips. It's the only kind of tea I drink these days."

"Anything is fine," Gardenia called as Frieda shuffled into the kitchen.

Tall bookcases stood against one wall, and on the other were two large, identically framed and matted portraits of Edna St. Vincent Millay and oddly, Fred Rogers of the *Mister Rogers' Neighborhood* TV show. A glass cabinet held the teacup collection that Frieda had mentioned, though she had already set out the cups and saucers they would use that afternoon. Through a far doorway was Frieda's bedroom, with a pile of clothing spilling out of a wicker laundry basket onto the bed. The largest window in the living room had a pleasing view of a stout hawthorn tree, not yet in bloom but that Gardenia suspected would be capable of providing a fine backdrop of bright pink flowers in May.

"I always put milk in my cup first, that's what the Brits do," Frieda said, pouring for herself. "Go ahead and fix yours any way you like."

"Binding one's tannins," Gardenia said as she reached for the milk jug and the teapot.

"Pardon?"

"That's what my husband and I used to call it. The milk in the tea binds the tannins and makes it easier on the stomach."

"*Used* to call it? Did you change your mind?"

"My husband's dead."

"Oh, sorry. I should have remembered that."

"It's OK." Gardenia got busy sipping her tea.

"Was it long ago? When he died?" Frieda started to help herself to the scones before offering them to Gardenia but corrected herself and stuck the plate out with a flourish.

"Two years," Gardenia said, reaching for a scone. "A heart attack. Sudden. He rode his bike and wasn't overweight. Or a smoker."

"But after two years, you must get used to him being gone."

"Yes and no. I mean, I said that line about 'binding tannins,' which

I hadn't thought of for a while. It hits you when you least expect it."

Gardenia broke off a large piece of the scone and stuffed it, jamless, in her mouth. This gave her face something to do besides crumple into tears.

"I wonder if you know anything much about the new hire?" Frieda asked.

"Dr. DuBarr?"

"Are there any *other* new hires? Well, you are. I'm glad we have a new administrative assistant. Doris Breen snapped at everyone, even the dean. I asked Arn many times to speak with her about it. I think he was afraid of her. You're not the snappy kind at all."

"Thanks, but you didn't feel like telling her yourself?" Gardenia finished off her tea to wash down the jamless scone.

"No way. I was in the middle of setting up a new series of poetry classes, and I needed her to do all the busywork with finding empty classrooms and putting descriptions on the website. I wasn't going to get on her bad side."

"Well, seems she is off enjoying life now, so maybe she doesn't need to snap at people. I can't imagine what it would feel like to get a huge inheritance, out of the blue."

"Didn't you get a nice lump sum from your husband's life insurance?" Frieda asked as she refilled her cup before pouring more for Gardenia. "That's one of the main benefits of having a husband, a second source of income. I'm forty-one. I'd consider getting married if I had the chance. You could remarry."

"I see that you have portraits of Edna St. Vincent Millay and Fred Rogers, side by side," Gardenia said, wanting to change the subject as she felt her throat fill with sadness. "My son and I watched *Mister*

Rogers' Neighborhood. There's something hypnotic about the way he talked to the audience." Frieda knew nothing about her life as Torre's wife and now as his widow, her life as Hans's mother, her life as Milo's grandmother! It was as if she and Frieda were from two different countries and did not speak the same language.

"I met Fred Rogers, in Pittsburgh," Frieda said. "I shook his hand. He looked at me as if he had never seen such an incredible person before. But I saw that he looked at the next woman in line the same way. And a little boy. And so on, for everybody in the line. Either he sees the holy in everyone or has no ability to discriminate between holy and horrible." Frieda poured the last dribble of tea into her cup.

"To separate wheat from chaff," Gardenia offered, bringing to mind slender, smiling Mr. Rogers flailing away at stacks of harvested stalks, bits of the straw sticking to his cardigan sweater. "You must have appreciated all the songs he wrote. Poetry, in its way."

"And he told me he liked me just the way I am."

At this Frieda's eyes glistened. Gardenia, startled, reached out to offer a comforting pat, but Frieda stood up and lurched to the kitchen, returning with a box of tissues.

"When he died I cried all day." Frieda blew her nose and stretched a fresh tissue over her eyes, like a burglar's mask, to mop up her tears.

Wait, Gardenia thought. I had just been talking about Torre's death, the subject quickly veering toward life insurance settlements rather than my loss, and now here I am, comforting Frieda as she blubbers over a dead TV personality.

"She's had a book published and another is on the way," Gardenia announced.

"Pardon?" Frieda blew her nose again.

"You asked what I know about Dr. DuBarr. I saw her résumé, and it said she's had a book published by Yale University Press."

"Oh yes, *her*. The dean said whoever replaced Gludger had to be well published. You see, some in the department are dragging their feet, dear as they may be. Working on the same manuscript for years," Frieda said.

"Dr. Wiggens?"

"How did you know?"

"A guess."

"Arnold and I have been friends ever since I joined the department six years ago. He convinced the tenure committee that I was a good catch." The caffeine in the strong tea had animated Frieda, who continued in a tone close to the definition of *rant*. "The others kept wanting me to teach poetry writing, but Arn stood up for me and said knowing how to teach *about* poetry was plenty. All those open mics, people standing up and reading a string of words that they call a poem. No meter, no rhyme, no stanzas even. At least my students can count out an iambic pentameter by the time I'm done with them. She's not married, is she?" Frieda crammed the spent tissues into a pocket of her corduroy pants.

"I haven't asked her directly but I don't think so." Gardenia started to pour some more tea for herself but the pot was empty. Frieda did not jump up to make more.

"Women like that, they attract men but find it's not as easy to keep them. More interested in themselves than anyone else."

"I don't know her well enough to say if that's the case." Gardenia scolded herself for being so interested in the relationship status of Frieda and Laurel and Arnold, as if she had stepped onto the set of a soap opera and needed backstory on all the other characters.

"Arn is a bachelor. Though when I first came here, he had this girlfriend, Maggie, who was around a lot. Came to some department parties. Big head of red hair. Didn't seem his type at all. Owned one of those shops that sell fancy tablecloths. I wonder what they talked about?"

"Sex?" Gardenia said.

"I don't think so. How could you keep a relationship going talking about *that*?" Frieda noisily slapped Gardenia's empty scone plate on top of her own and picked up the teapot.

"I wasn't thinking *talk* about sex. Maybe they had a sex thing going that kept them together."

"I don't think so," Frieda said. "I mean, Arn is such a cultured man. And he loves that dog."

What Leroy had to do with the sexual appetite of Arnold Wiggens, Gardenia wasn't sure. "Indeed," she said, as if channeling Arnold himself, and stood up to deliver her cup and saucer to the kitchen counter.

"Don't feel you have to rush off," Frieda said.

"Thank you for the tea and scones, but I do need to get home soon and work in my yard before it gets dark." She had no more time for a tea party that featured so many small self-centered acts by Dr. Frieda Hamm and odd references to Arnold Wiggens and his love life, even though she was the one who had lobbed sex into the conversation.

The late-afternoon April sunshine made Gardenia squint when she left the dimly lit front hallway. On her way to her parked car, she passed the queue for the food bank at the Baptist church. A woman in the line wore an REI jacket identical to Gardenia's. That could be me, Gardenia thought. Without this job, I would be edging closer to the food bank line.

The kind Christopher at Lucky Produce had been a one-time food bank for her, she realized, but soon her paychecks would kick in and she would never need such help again.

Chapter Eleven

"Arn, would you slice up those cherry tomatoes and the avocado and some of the kalamata olives? I always make Greek salad for large groups."

Frieda spoke to Arnold over her shoulder as she stood at the stove, stirring a pot of risotto.

"Cheap and cheerful, as our friends the Brits would say." Arnold began slicing the small tomatoes with a paring knife, first rolling up the sleeves of the black shirt he pulled out of his closet for special occasions.

"We do have to economize, don't we, Arn?" Frieda went on, hearing perhaps the word *cheap* but not *cheerful*, nor understanding the reference to the Britishism. "People don't realize what kind of salaries we make." Frieda waved her wooden spoon for emphasis, flicking some grains of arborio rice onto the counter but not bothering to wipe them up.

"To-*mah*-toes, done and dusted," Arnold muttered as he swept the lot into an orange plastic salad bowl.

"I dust, on Saturdays but especially before a party."

"I didn't mean to question your housekeeping. Just another phrase the Brits use."

"Whatever. But thanks for coming early to help, Arn. Well, nothing stopping us from starting on the wine." Frieda retrieved the Malbec that Arnold had chosen as his contribution to the drinks table and handed the bottle to him with a corkscrew. "I always love having a man around to open the wine."

Arnold poured two glasses. Frieda leaned against the kitchen counter as coquettishly as a woman could manage while wearing an oversized checked apron with a brown stain of what looked like a splash of futilely laundered barbecue sauce.

"Cheers." She reached up to clink Arnold's glass. "To our sixth year in the department together."

"I've had good luck with this vintner," Arnold replied as a way to vault over any emotions that had been simmering in Frieda during the fifteen minutes they had inhabited her kitchen together. Six years? Was that all? It seemed as if there had never been a time when Dr. Frieda Hamm had not been scurrying in and out of her office. Or was it the effort of politely disregarding her attempts to become "better friends"—a phrase Frieda invoked often—that made it seem longer?

"Arn, I may not have told you directly how much your support has meant to me." She looked up at him with moist gray-green eyes. "Having an ally in the department. You have always been so kind to me."

"Onward to the alligator pear." Arnold put his glass down and slit the thick wrinkled skin of an avocado, to parry what he feared was a romantic thrust from Frieda.

"And did your mother tell you I bought her a ticket to the new play at the Lakeshore Theatre? She agreed that I should get one for you."

"Ah, did she?" Oh blast. His interfering mother!

"I mean, I thought it would be fun to go together," Frieda said, stepping closer to Arnold, as if this would change his opinion about the news. "Your mother and I are becoming good friends."

"And I leave it to her to make her own friends and let me make mine," Arnold muttered. The doorbell rang.

"I'm betting it's Dodge," Frieda said as she untied the stained apron, "and his wife. I never can remember her name."

The voice at the entry that greeted Frieda was not that of Dodge, nor of his wife.

It was Laurel's.

"Nice location for an apartment. You can walk to work, can't you? Here, I didn't have time to make anything, but I brought cupcakes from that bakery near campus. They were just about to close for the day, so I got a deal on what they had left."

Arnold realized that Dr. Laurel DuBarr had slipped onto the same sliver of planet that he occupied.

He would add the diced avocado to the pile of sliced tomatoes in the orange plastic bowl.

He would move on to slicing olives.

He would saunter into the living room with his glass of Malbec in one hand and the uncorked bottle in the other.

He would nod hello to Laurel and, with any luck, his face would not flush at the pleasure of seeing her, and no one would hear the mad thumping of his heart.

"There you are. The cook's assistant," Laurel said as she walked into the kitchen. "Assigned to olive duty?"

"I suspect that no Greek would trouble himself or herself with the slicing of olives," Arnold offered, though he had no clue whether this was true. This was the first time he had seen Laurel dressed in a nonprofessional manner. Her tight white jeans stopped just above her ankles, a filmy blouse hugged her narrow waist, and her tan high-heeled sandals made her a tad taller than he.

"They'd say, 'That's the pits,'" Laurel said.

A honk of laughter. Were he to be one hundred percent honest, this is how Arnold would have described the sound that Laurel made in appreciation of her own joke. Never had he heard her laugh like this before, their previous conversations apparently not conducive to such levity.

"How clever," he said, and mixed the salad ingredients vaguely with a wooden spoon.

"Thanks. Always nice when someone gets my sense of humor."

"Indeed. May I pour you a glass of wine?"

"No thanks. I'm drinking water tonight. It's my week for a detox." She yanked open cabinet doors until she found a tumbler and rummaged in Frieda's fridge to find some bottled water. Arnold stood with his hands drooping in front of him like the forepaws of a patient kangaroo, unable to wash the olive juice from his fingers because Laurel had chosen to lean against the sink to sip her water.

"I never ask my guests to help me cook," she whispered. "Oh, wait. Maybe you're used to helping Frieda in the kitchen?"

"Nothing like that," Arnold said, "we're just colleagues."

"And you're sure she feels the same way? I hate that, when you have to show up at work and someone is waiting there with a crush on you and you have to pretend you don't notice."

"As I said, Frieda and I are . . ." Arnold began, but the doorbell rang, this time delivering enough guests to produce a stew of cheerful greetings.

"Sounds like the party has started." Laurel ambled from the kitchen with her tumbler of water.

Frieda returned to the kitchen and announced, "Everyone's here but Gardenia. Oh, and Dodge." Switching to a whisper she said, "I offered Laurel some wine, but she wouldn't accept even half a glass. Something about detox. Some people are so stuck on their latest health fad." She scooped the risotto into a large crockery bowl.

"She's driving herself home," Arnold said and picked up the orange bowl. "I hope the salad is OK."

"It looks fine. I like cooking with you."

Once again the doorbell saved him.

"I'll get it," he said.

A bright pink blouse set off the color in Gardenia's cheeks. "Hi! This is Lex Ohashi. Lex, Arnold Wiggens."

"Nice to meet you. The Chaucer scholar, I hear?" Lex said.

"I told him how you get undergrads turned on to *The Canterbury Tales*," Gardenia said as she hung a black fringed shawl on the coatrack by the front door.

"You are also a university teacher?" Arnold thought he had seen this Lex before though was not sure where. He was surprised to see Gardenia with a man, particularly one that many would describe as *hot*. The fact that Gardenia could attract such a fellow made Arnold feel that he had not judged her correctly at all. He had imagined that she was a kindhearted, if depressed and grieving, widow when here she was, managing to date someone distinguished and handsome.

"No, engineer by trade. For buildings and such," Lex said.

"His name is on the plaque by the new campus chapel," Gardenia said.

"Ah, that's why you look familiar," Arnold said.

"I was around UNW during construction."

"The chapel turned out well. Much admired," Arnold said.

"Well, can't say working with those architects was the high point of my career, but yes, the building is fairly cool, so that's good." Lex slid a bottle of brandy among the grove of wine bottles on a card table.

Dean Dodge and his wife arrived last.

Frieda had set out six folding chairs to amplify the seating that was available on the small sofa, a wicker rocker, and a primly uncomfortable upholstered chair. In the middle of the carpet she had arranged four plump cushions, suggesting perhaps that the younger, more limber faculty members encamp there. But when it was evident that no one was going to sit on the floor, Arnold gathered up the pillows and stacked them in the corner.

"Oh, Arn, thank you. What was I thinking, that any of these people would sit on the floor?" Frieda hung on his arm, her face flushed from the Malbec. "I knew you'd help me out with the party. It's so much easier when there's someone else who cares about how it all turns out."

"No one has particularly grand expectations of a department party," Arnold said.

"But everyone has a good time at my parties, if I do say so myself," Frieda said.

Standing with a limp paper plate of the Greek salad, Frieda's risotto, and lumpia prepared by Dodge's wife, Arnold surveyed the room much as he had done throughout his life when two or more people were gathered together. He had understood long ago that he was not intended to be the center of any social event but instead one of those on the perimeter. He reasoned, though, that it was far more enlightening to observe than to be part of the exhausting small talk and banter, which became louder and louder as the wine bottles emptied.

Dodge had taken up residence on the sofa and was holding forth to two graduate students who had claimed the rocker and the upholstered chair. The dean was clearly pleased to pontificate even at a party. His wife, looking like a decorated birthday cake in her extravagant full-skirted dress, fetched him more lumpia, refilled his wineglass, and patted his knee solicitously as an erstwhile nurse might do. Arnold wouldn't mention the unpleasant conversation that had transpired at Dodge's home.

No one else knows, apparently, of my possible demotion, he thought. Dodge wouldn't be so low as to announce it at a social gathering.

While Lex was examining Frieda's bookcases, Laurel approached and pulled a fat volume from the top shelf, riffling through it and, to Arnold's astonishment, making some comment that caused Lex to laugh. Distinguished-and-Handsome fetched Laurel a glass of wine that she was not supposed to be drinking but accepted nonetheless.

"You're a watcher too." Gardenia slipped into the space beside Arnold. "My husband used to tell me to stop staring, when we were at parties, but I couldn't help it. For me it's more fun to watch than to be part of it all."

"I could not agree more," Arnold said.

With a plastic fork Gardenia speared a piece of the avocado that Arnold had diced. "I recently met Lex at a coffee shop, and we ran into each other at a drum concert. This morning he called, and I asked him to come with me. I hope that's all right."

"Significant others are welcome."

"Oh, he's not *significant* at all." With her rosy cheeks and dark eyes, Gardenia Pitkin resembled a fetching marsupial from some children's picture book, even more so when she smiled to show the gap between her teeth.

"I just hope our hostess doesn't have a party game in reserve," Arnold said, sensing a change of subject was in order.

"You've got that right. Can you believe that Torre and I went to a party once where the hostess brought out Twister? No one was brave enough to refuse. So there we all were, grappling with each other on this piece of plastic. But I wouldn't worry. The room's got that healthy buzz you want as a hostess."

Silently Arnold stood beside Gardenia as they finished their lumpia and Greek salad. Laurel had been beside the bookcase chatting and laughing with this Lex fellow longer than Arnold wanted her to. Finally she approached the sofa, where Angelina scooted over to make room for her.

"Laurel seems to be fitting in," Gardenia said. "I assume she would be a tenure-track candidate for Gludger's spot?"

"That is a possibility," Arnold said. "The dean invited her to present a college seminar on her latest book."

"At least she's not going to perish," Gardenia said. "what with her publishing. Though just between you and me, I can't understand what she's writing about. Though I know that must mean I'm not as smart as she is."

Gardenia made a face as if imitating someone arrogantly superior. So clever was her miming, Arnold started to laugh. He stopped himself as he realized she was mocking Laurel.

"It's a matter of getting used to the topic. Some would call it the jargon of the profession."

"I much prefer learning about the old guys and what they wrote," Gardenia went on, "like the Chaucer that you teach. At least we know they've lasted a long time, so there's some reason to study them. The newer books, who knows? Are they too modern for us to understand, or is it one of those emperor's new clothes things?" She shrugged. "I'll take your plate and throw it away with mine."

Just as Gardenia left for the kitchen, Laurel stood up from where she was wedged beside Angelina and joined Arnold.

"Don't see you mingling much," she said.

"Seems the group is adequately mingled without me." Arnold sipped from his wineglass, which proved to be empty.

"That guy who came with Hyacinth? He doesn't seem her type. He said he was in a conga line with her. How weird is that?"

"Gardenia." Frieda had joined them.

"What?" Laurel, in her platform sandals, bent down toward Frieda.

"Her name is Gardenia, not Hyacinth."

"Oh, that's right. I knew it was some kind of plant."

"*Your* name is a plant," Frieda said. "There's a row of laurels in front of the apartment building. They have to be whacked back every year." Clutching two empty wine bottles by their necks, she stomped into the kitchen.

"Oh man," Laurel said. "I've been here an hour and a half. Do you think I could excuse myself now?"

"I would guess you could. No one's toes seem in danger of being stepped on," Arnold said.

"What? Oh, I guess that's funny."

Arnold, embarrassed that his turn of phrase did not bring instant appreciation and annoyed that he had not edited himself, did not have a chance to reply, for at that moment Frieda returned from the kitchen.

"Cupcakes, come and get your cupcakes!" Frieda said, holding out the bakery box.

"We'll stay long enough to have one each, and we're out of here, OK?" Laurel whispered.

Ah, the frisson of the first-person plural pronoun!

Arnold wondered for a moment if she was using the royal "we" and decided she was not. He jammed a cupcake into his mouth.

When Arnold thanked Frieda and said good-bye, she replied, with a look of disappointment and even pain, "Oh, I thought maybe you'd stay behind and help with the dishes."

"He *is* your guest, not your manservant," Laurel said. "And you're using paper plates, anyway."

Not the kindest of words, Arnold thought, but oh well. He followed Laurel out the door, down the three flights of stairs, and into the fragrant April evening.

"Two of those, and much obliged," Arnold said to the waiter at the nearby pub that Laurel had chosen for an after-party drink.

"Two Windy Ridge? You got it. Excellent choice. One of my favorite ales."

The server nodded at Arnold and watched Laurel as she studied the late-night happy hour menu. Maybe the young man recognized her—a UNW student who had seen Dr. DuBarr sway along the campus pathways? Or was he simply unable to ignore her pale beauty in the low light of the pub?

"Anything else for you?"

"Yep, an order of the fries," Laurel said.

"You got it. And something to eat for you, sir?"

Arnold pulled the menu back from the edge of the table where he had placed it for the waiter's retrieval. If Laurel was going to eat something, perhaps he should, though he was not the least hungry after avocados and tomatoes and olives and lumpia and the hastily scarfed cupcake. "I'll have the small mixed green salad."

"Sure. We have ranch, thousand island, Caesar, oil and vinegar."

"The latter."

"OK, perfect. Two of the Windy Ridge ales, an order of fries, and a small mixed green with the oil and vinegar."

"Cute kid," Laurel said when the server was out of earshot. "Reminds me of a student I had a few years back. I kept thinking, What will you look like when you're forty? From the looks of the guys at my twentieth high school reunion, he won't stay cute."

"*He was as fresh as is the month of May*," Arnold quoted.

"What? Oh, something from Chaucer. Cool that you can come up with a line like that."

"Not all that surprising considering how many hours of my brief passage on the planet I have spent on Mr. Chaucer."

"And you're OK with that? I mean, we all know he's important and worth studying, but don't you run out of things to say about him?" Laurel asked.

The waiter slid a tall glass of ale in front of each of them—Laurel seemed to have put her detox regimen aside for another day. Arnold hoisted his glass. "*Salut*. Ah, that's a good question, but the answer could take us well past the end of happy hour."

Justifying Chaucer to her would be like asking him to justify his complex yet enduring affection for his mother.

"OK." Laurel's dispatch of her first swallow of ale could only be called a gulp.

"An extra plate for each of you, in case you want to share." The waiter deposited the salad and the platter of fries in the middle of the table.

Laurel squeezed a pool of ketchup at the edge of the mound of fries.

No one ever said that attractive women should not enjoy fries, Arnold thought, nor was it written that such women should not gather several in a bundle and eat them lustily after dipping them in ketchup. The sight of Laurel tucking in so eagerly and swigging Windy Ridge ale was both mesmerizing and disconcerting.

"So what is it like to come up for tenure at the University of the Northwest? You were pretty sure you'd be OK?" she asked.

"Sometimes they refuse a candidate, but I don't recall being that concerned." And this was the truth. After he had served his years as an assistant professor, no one else in the department had the slightest interest in teaching Chaucer or Middle English, and his classes were nearly always full to capacity because they were required for an English degree. Almost as soon as he was granted tenure, however, the siren call of computer science and business majors began to pull students away from the liberal arts.

"I've got a fairly awesome résumé, if I do say so myself. The students like my classes. Takes a while for them to get what I'm talking about. I have to be sure I don't make them feel like idiots while I'm trying." Laurel pushed the platter, with its remaining half dozen fries and splattering of ketchup, to the side of the table. "Can't believe I ate all those fries. Guess because I ran five miles today. What do you do for cardio?"

"Shank's mare," Arnold said.

"Whose mare?"

"Shank's. It means walking."

At this Laurel threw her head back and laughed, her filly's throat white except for a tiny speck of ketchup. "Arnold, you are incredible. I mean, it's like you're from some BBC show, the way you talk. And you're American, aren't you?"

"Born and raised in the great Midwestern college town of Champaign-Urbana, Illinois. Only child of a chemistry professor." I am ready and willing to share more of my upbringing, he thought, should she wish to learn more about me.

But at that moment the server appeared with the bill. As Arnold reached for it, Laurel said, "Nope, we're splitting this," and slipped her credit card on top of his. "I'm a woman who pays my own way."

Escorting Laurel back to her car, parked a block from Frieda's building, Arnold scolded himself for imagining that this might be an opportunity for a quick kiss on the cheek or an affectionate hug—Laurel is a colleague, not a romantic possibility, you fool! And what about sexual harassment?

But swiftly his memory carried him back to the first time he had kissed his ex-girlfriend, Maggie. It had been outside the tiny elevator of the parking garage across the street from Benaroya Hall, after he had taken her to hear the Seattle Men's Chorus. His tweed sport coat had not been warm enough for the December evening. He'd been eager to get into the car and turn on the heater. Maggie, however, cozy in her down coat, had seemed in no hurry. As they stepped off the elevator, she'd reached up, clamped her arms around his neck, and kissed him full on the mouth.

He'd been surprised though not unhappy about this development. The relationship it led to had been full of aggravations as well as full-mouthed kisses and all the rest. It had ended after two confusing years.

"Hel-*lo*?" Laurel jingled her car keys in front of Arnold to get his attention. "I said, let's get together sometime."

"Pardon me. Yes, why not? I'd like to hear more about your book. Won't you join Leroy and me at the Magnuson Park off-leash area tomorrow morning?" Arnold heard himself ask. "By Lake Washington."

"Cool. Maybe someplace I can go running. But don't expect me to be out and about before ten."

"That suits us just fine." Which was not exactly true. Leroy was always raring to go on a Sunday morning. They usually were at the dog park no later than eight thirty. Well, they could leave later. Leroy could have a leisurely frolic and would be ready to snooze in the Volvo by the time Laurel arrived.

She nudged his arm playfully before climbing into the driver's seat of her Escort sedan. "See you tomorrow."

Arnold drove slowly back to his apartment, concerned about the effect of a glass of Malbec and another of Windy Ridge. At the dog park he would ask Laurel's advice on PowerPoint. In appreciation for her help, he would regale her with all he knew of the tenure process and show her the scenic delights of Magnuson Park. Mount Rainier might even be visible to the south, at the far end of Lake Washington.

Theirs would be a mutual aid society, not unheard of among academic colleagues, nothing more.

And yet it *could* evolve into something more, Arnold told himself. No need to rule out any possibility.

Chapter Twelve

THE MAGNUSON PARK off-leash dog area was a canine circus on Sunday mornings. Labs and Rottweilers and Rhodesian ridgebacks and beagles and Shiba Inus careened along the muddy paths. For this outing with Susie, Gardenia put on a pair of black rubber boots that had once belonged to Hans and a tattered burgundy windbreaker that she used for gardening, thus becoming a comrade with the other drably dressed women who made no attempt to fix themselves up for the dog park.

One could say that we dog owners, too, are off-leash, in a fashion sense, she thought.

Gardenia took Susie to a fenced-off patch with a sign that read: *For shy, small, and elderly dogs.* She joined a young woman with two snuffling black pugs and another with a shivering Chihuahua. Susie sniffed her way around the clumps of scrubby grass, peeing happily. The April morning was spicy, the blooming of the last cherry trees and magnolias and apple trees all converging. The blue sky, with mounds of white clouds, promised a clear and maybe even warm day. Toward the east the Cascades still showed a generous icing of snow.

"He's almost *elderly*, and is *small* compared to other breeds, though

I can't vouch for the *shy* attribute."

Without turning around, Gardenia knew who was speaking.

"Dr. Wiggens!"

Arnold waved from where he stood, talking to the owner of the pugs, and unsnapped Leroy's leash before joining Gardenia.

"Please, *Arnold* to you, even when beckoning from across the *small, shy, and elderly* area."

"OK. I don't think I've ever seen you here before."

"We don't come often, as it requires some travel time."

Arnold wore a canvas hat with a shallow brim. Coiled around his neck was what appeared to be a hand-knit scarf. Underneath his unzipped jacket was a tailored gray shirt, similar to the one he had sported the previous evening at the department party. He had not shaved, which made him seem less turgidly academic, and even—could it be?—slightly sexy.

Gardenia said, "That's my Susie, over in the far corner."

"A fine-looking dachshund indeed."

Leroy, nose to the ground, traced the edge of the enclosure.

"Isn't it great, the way dogs are so in the moment? Nothing on their minds other than whatever is there for them to sniff. No worries about what's going on in anyone else's life." Gardenia discovered two individually wrapped chocolates in her pocket. "Oh, where did these come from? Here."

She offered one to Arnold and stuffed the other in her mouth. He did the same. They stood side by side, silenced by the jumbo truffles, their gazes tracking the movements of their lowriders, just as Gardenia had once watched Hans as he romped around playgrounds. Here I am in my grubby jacket, my hair brushed but not washed this morning, with no attempt to look nice for anyone, Gardenia thought, and I don't mind at all that I ran into this fellow Arnold Wiggens. He seemed not the least self-conscious about his clumsy chewing of the delicious chocolate truffle.

"*It was a lover and his lass / With a hey, and a ho, and a hey nonino / That o'er the green corn-field did pass / In the springtime, the only pretty ring time / When birds do sing, hey ding a ding, ding / Sweet lovers love the spring.*" Arnold had switched to a chesty theatrical voice and delivered Shakespeare's lines with a straight back and flinging of the arms, so that Gardenia stepped aside just in time to avoid being bonked on the face. "How fortunate I am to have poetic lines to attach to a day like this. Thank you, Miss Mabel Stuyvesant, fifth-grade teacher."

A poem rose from Gardenia's own literary database, from the children's poetry collection she had read as a child and later, to Hans: "*Sound the flute! / Now it's mute. / Birds delight / Day and night; / Nightingale / In the dale, / Lark in sky, / Merrily . . .*"

"*. . . Merrily, merrily, to welcome in the year,*" Arnold finished for her. "Ah yes, by our dear friend Mr. Blake."

"*Little boy, / Full of joy; / Little girl, / Sweet and small; / Cock does crow, / So do you; Merry voice, / Infant noise, / Merrily, merrily, to welcome in the year,*" they recited together.

"Maybe we read the same poetry book when we were children?" Gardenia said. "*Childworld: Our Favorite Poems?*"

"Indeed. A dark blue cover strong enough to withstand the decades. The book is still in my mother's bookcase, waiting to be read by a grandchild."

Gardenia would not mention that she was already reading some of the easier poems to *her* grandchild. Maybe Arnold's obvious interest in Laurel DuBarr was the result of wanting, before it was too late, to settle down and have a child.

"You are adjusting to the complexities of the Department of English?" Arnold smiled and dabbed at the corners of his mouth with a crumpled handkerchief.

"That first week of class was pretty crazy, all those stressed-out students. But now I'm doing OK."

"You seem at ease with the average undergraduate angst. Doris Breen could be a trifle on the impatient side."

"I heard that Doris wasn't just *impatient* but kind of a battle-axe," Gardenia said.

"Ah."

Kind Arnold was not going to carry this line of conversation any further. Gardenia scolded herself for revealing her tendency to gossip to a man who was, first of all, her boss and, second of all, a human being clearly of more exalted and generous nature than she. Embarrassed, she searched for some other topic. "Have you ever seen a dorgi?"

"*A dorgi?*"

"One of the Queen's corgis got together with Princess Margaret's dachshund, and voilà."

"And are the ears dachshund or corgi?" Arnold asked.

"Pointed ears. But the coat resembles Leroy's. Ah, here they are."

Susie trotted up, Leroy right behind her.

"Looks like our two are friends." Gardenia stroked Leroy's firm, shiny back. Arnold crouched down and offered his fist for Susie to sniff, but she pulled back and bared her teeth.

"A fine imitation of a wolf, Miss Scruffy Dachshund."

"Oh, I'm sorry."

"I'm sure we'll become friends over time." He checked his watch.

"Am I keeping you from something?" Gardenia asked.

"I agreed to meet someone here at ten."

"Isn't it past ten by now? I'll be on my way."

"Please, don't let me rush you," Arnold said, but from his nervous smile Gardenia could tell that he *did* want to rush her.

Was he meeting a woman? Frieda maybe?

"I thought you said you'd be letting your dog run around!" yelled Laurel as she picked her way around a mud puddle. "I was over there in that open area."

"Sorry." Arnold snapped on Leroy's leash. "Laurel is new to Seattle, as you know, so I offered to show her around Magnuson."

"Oh, hi," Laurel said to Gardenia. "I didn't realize you'd be here."

"Arnold and I just ran into each other. I come here sometimes with *my* dachshund." Gardenia picked Susie up, not wanting her to growl or nip at Laurel. "But it's time for us to head home."

"I felt pretty ridiculous, walking around over in that field without a dog," Laurel said, pulling the elastic band off her ponytail. "Like some kind of weirdo voyeur."

Oh please, don't fall for her, Gardenia wanted to whisper to Arnold. She's hanging out with you because she wants you to put in a good word about the tenure-track job. Yes, she's got those long legs and that blonde hair and all those publications, but you deserve someone better.

Or maybe you're better off on your own, so you don't have to worry about the person you care about sleeping around—like Princess Margaret's dachshund.

Or my son's wife.

Chapter Thirteen

PREPARING FOR THE barbecue at her dear friend Sylvie's that evening, Gardenia plucked her eyebrows, snapped on her dental tray with whitening gel to spruce up her teeth, and ironed a cotton tunic that she had bought several years before, from an online fair-trade site established to help widows in India earn a living.

How are you ladies doing? she wondered as she pulled the top over her head. What are your days like as you raise your children without a husband nearby? What's it like, crouching over a sewing machine, day after sweltering day, making tops like this for widows like me to wear to a backyard barbecue?

Our lives are so different, but you know what it's like to have lost a husband, she thought, something we have in common that Sylvie and I don't.

Gardenia arrived to find most of the guests gathered in the backyard. A large glass vase on the beverage table was crammed with narcissi, and instead of matching plates, Sylvie had set out a stack of assorted vintage china, cleverly collected from thrift stores and garage sales. Doug, her husband, stood in command of the majestic gas barbecue grill. I'll bet that cost as much as a month of my salary, Gardenia thought.

"There you are." Sylvie hugged her and poured her a glass of chardonnay, no doubt chosen from a list of good, reasonably priced wines posted on some connoisseur's list. "Oh, Bruce—I guess you don't know Gardenia?"

A balding man about Gardenia's age extended his hand.

"Bruce McPhee. My wife and Sylvie went to high school together."

"Denie, you would have loved Janine, but unfortunately, she passed." Sylvie put an arm around Bruce's shoulders.

Passed. Maybe it was a result of being recently plunked into a school environment where talk of *passing* was always hanging in the air, but for a second Gardenia imagined that Janine had just finished some sort of qualifying exam. She almost asked what Janine was studying when she realized that she had just been told that Bruce's wife was dead.

"I am so sorry," Gardenia said.

"Thank you. And I hear that we're in the same boat, in that regard."

"Yes. Two years ago." Gardenia looked down as Bruce offered a sympathetic gaze.

"I'm off to get the Indonesian rice salad on the table," Sylvie said. "I made it for you, Denie. I know you always like it."

Don't leave me here with this man! Gardenia almost shouted as her friend left for the kitchen. This Bruce seemed anybody's idea of a solid, respectable, dependable middle-aged guy: Mid-fifties. Hair clipped short to keep the bare spots from contrasting sharply with the still lush patches. Clear blue eyes behind progressives, attractive youthful frames with a touch of Euro style. A cotton shirt tucked into khakis. A soft paunch but generally fit body. Brown boat shoes.

But I am not, not, *not* interested, Gardenia thought, if this is an attempt at a setup.

"Let me get you some more white."

As Bruce nearly grabbed her empty glass, Gardenia was shuttled back to the days when some nice boy would fetch her a glass of punch at a high school dance. Oh, how exhausting it had been as a teenager and a young woman, trying to fend off some males and yet attract others! A benefit of married life was the slender gold band on your left ring finger, a powerful talisman against being hit on. Though the world was filled, if you believed TV and movies and novels, with philandering married people.

And my daughter-in-law may be one of them, she thought but then flashed on Torre. Or may *not* be one of them, she corrected herself.

It's *my* problem that I imagine zebras.

Bruce presented the refilled glass with a smile. "How do you know Sylvie?" he asked.

"Esme was in co-op preschool with our son, Hans."

"Janine had lots of friends from those days. When our two were little."

"How old are they now?"

"Let's see, I have to do a little math. Audrey is thirty and Sam is twenty-seven. And yours?"

"He just turned twenty-four. Same as Esme. You must have grandchildren by now?" Gardenia asked.

"Unfortunately, no. Oh man, I wonder if I'll be able to enjoy a grandchild without my Janine beside me."

"I think you will. A grandchild is a wonderful thing," Gardenia said.

Bruce ran the liver-spotted back of his hand over his eyes. He wiped some tears with a dainty cocktail napkin. "You never know when it's going to happen. Easier to cry in public if you're a woman. Nobody wants a guy to weep and wail and carry on. They want you to hurry up and get over it—'Good God, man, it's been nearly three years. Time to move on, old chap.' But it's not that easy, is it?"

"No, it isn't."

Oh, the odd times she had burst into tears! On seeing a display of the applesauce that Torre liked at the grocery store, or finding a pair of his beat-up underwear in the rag bag, or discovering his handwriting on a voided check in the bottom of the junk drawer.

Thankfully, Doug called, "Salmon's ready!"

"Denie, so glad you could come." Doug leaned his six-plus feet over so he could kiss her cheek, his hands out of commission in thick orca-motif oven mitts. "Sylvie said you were waffling about coming, but I guess her powers of persuasion worked."

"I always enjoy your parties," Gardenia said, which was true. It was just the jolly atmosphere and everyone else's coupledom that was hard.

Challenging.

Sometimes even excruciating.

She found an empty chair by a tall boxwood planted in a terra-cotta container. The grilled salmon was charred to just the right degree on the outside, the orange flesh still moist. One of the male guests was fiddling with an old-fashioned boom box perched on a stool near the back door so that it spewed Aretha singing "Respect."

"May I pull up a chair?" Bruce asked. "I don't know about you, but it's kind of rare for me to eat with other people these days. And to eat home cooking. I'm looking forward to this."

"I always cook something for myself from scratch," Gardenia

declared, not wanting to be lumped into the microwave-lasagna tribe of single adults.

"Well, good on ya. I always let Janine do most the cooking, even though I knew it wasn't PC. She was so much better than I was, so I didn't get in there and learn. Wish I had."

"It's never too late," Gardenia said. "All the cooking shows on YouTube. And tons of good cookbooks, with pictures."

"Sylvie said I should sign up for a cooking class. A way to meet people. But I don't want to *have* to show up. I never know what my mood will be. Know what I mean? Though I wouldn't mind it if someone wanted to give me one-on-one cooking lessons."

Gardenia focused on extracting tiny salmon bones. Was Bruce implying that she would want to coach him on the mysteries of braising and sautéing? What cheek! Sylvie, for all her good intentions, imagines Bruce and me to be two of the same minority, Gardenia thought. It's as if we have the same color of skin or speak the same dialect. But just because we have widowhood in common, it doesn't mean we share anything else.

"Gardenia," Bruce murmured, "I know we've only just met, but I have a favor to ask." He parked his empty plate on the ground below the plastic lawn chair. "I want to make a deal with you."

Gardenia became interested in a chunk of red potato saturated with vinaigrette.

"I know, that sounds like a come-on. You'll have to forgive me. I never was good with small talk. Always let Janine take care of that, and now I'm paying the price. I can see people wince when I approach, but what can I do? If I don't want to be a lonely old codger, I have to get out and be with people and learn to chat."

"Well" was all that Gardenia could think to say. She understood the desperate sadness in his eyes, but what was he thinking, that he could ask her a favor, though they had only just met? Was he proposing something kinky, some sort of arrangement for mutual sexual release? She stood up with her now-empty plate.

"No, wait, please. I'm being forward, but I have to ask." He took her plate, shoved it under the chair on top of his own, and gestured for her to sit down.

"It's hearing her name," he cooed huskily. "I want to talk about her. Tell people things I remember about her. Go back over stories about Janine, again and again. But no one gets it. They flinch when I start to talk about her. Creeps them out. Know what I mean?"

"Yes."

Bruce was absolutely right. She had a deep need to talk about Torre, to share all kinds of little details and memories, to fill others in on who he was, and keep him alive this way. Not even sweet Sylvie thought to ask Gardenia to tell her stories about Torre. It was hard to talk about him even with Hans. The memories she'd bring up would not be those that Hans wanted to hear. If it was something they'd shared as a family, Hans would correct her, saying he remembered the event in a different way.

"I knew it, I knew you'd understand." Bruce grabbed her hand, not suggestively, or gallantly, but beseechingly. A grain of Indonesian rice salad was stuck to his cheek.

Gardenia pressed her lips together to suppress a chuckle. How consumed we humans can be by emotion or desire, she thought. And yet even when we are desperately sad and grieving, our bodies carry on, hearts beating, intestines digesting, throats swallowing, gallbladders churning out bile, stomachs demanding food that can adhere ignobly to one's face.

"We could take turns, you see," Bruce said as Gardenia pulled her hand away. "Just agree to listen to each other, say ten minutes at a time? You talk about your husband, anything you want to say"—he had not asked Torre's name—"and I'll talk about Janine. No apologies, no holding back. A form of group therapy, you might say."

"I'll think about it."

The thought of having the chance to indulge in all that she'd like to say about Torre, just to say his name over and over to someone else, was appealing.

"Let's exchange cell numbers and I'll call you tomorrow, OK? And we could start by doing it over the phone? And if it feels good, we could move on to doing it in person."

Gardenia gasped. Had anyone overheard this easily misconstrued conversation?

"I'd better see if Sylvie needs help." Gardenia stood up and headed to the kitchen, where Sylvie was lifting a formidable chocolate cake from a pink bakery box.

"You and Bruce seemed to have a lot to talk about," Sylvie said.

"Remember in the old days, when the store-bought cakes had that awful lard frosting?" Gardenia chirped, wanting to quickly change the subject. "But kids always liked it."

The two friends were silently admiring the cake, Gardenia glad to have a distraction from more comments about Bruce, when a thin, crackly voice called from the front door, "Anybody home?"

"In here!" Sylvie called back, and said to Gardenia, "Doug's mom. I invited her. Pretty amazing, isn't it, that I'd invite my mother-in-law to a party with my friends?"

"She's a cool lady."

"That she is, but I'll tell you the truth. If I invite her over now and then when I have a group, I don't have to find time for just the three of us, or worse, just the *two* of us. What can I say? She's my mother-in-law. We don't have much in common besides Doug and Esme."

Just as Caitlin's parents, the affluent Curlews, have almost nothing in common with me except our perfect grandson, Gardenia thought.

Frances swung her bike helmet from her wrist as she hugged Sylvie and kissed her cheek. She turned to Gardenia.

"I'm Frances, Doug's mom. I think we've met?"

"Yes, a while ago. At Thanksgiving."

"That's right. You're the pie baker."

"I do tend to bring pies," Gardenia said. *Tends to bring pies:* If I joined an internet dating service, which I'm not planning to do, would I include that line in my profile?

"I remember the crust," Frances went on. "I've tried all my bloomin' adult life to make pie crust, and it has never come out as well as that. I think you wrote down the recipe for me, but I didn't ever try it. More's the pity."

"I could give it to you again," Gardenia said.

"If you have a minute, before you go. Now, where's that rascal son of mine?"

Frances patted Gardenia's arm and deposited her bike helmet and cycling gloves on the countertop near the microwave. She was in her early eighties but wiry and fit, her calves sculpted with sinewy cyclist muscles, her arms in the sleeveless jersey taut and freckled. Her hair, a dull brown-gray, was curly and moist from its time stashed under the helmet. She walked with a bounce in her step that made her look much younger from the back, when you couldn't see the deep creases in her face and her eyelids sagging like an iguana's.

That's where I'm headed, Gardenia thought, an elderly widow with the occasional invitation to my son's home, and a list of jolly hobbies and activities meant to help me pass the last years of my life productively and hold off desperate loneliness.

"How long has it been since Doug's dad died?" Gardenia asked Sylvie, who was easing slices of cake onto dessert plates.

"Morris? Gee, a long time now. Maybe twenty-five years? Frances wasn't much older than you were when you lost Torre."

Gardenia forgave Sylvie for the twinge this remark caused and delivered the pieces of cake to the guests arranged around the back patio. Frances was now in the coveted half-hidden chair by the boxwood, forking up salmon and making Bruce laugh with her animated conversation. Would Bruce ask Frances about taking turns listening to stories of dead spouses? Gardenia wondered. Was he perhaps suggesting a threesome?

Gardenia busied herself with carting the leftover platters of food from the buffet table to the kitchen, thus avoiding having to talk with anyone. It's like a limb that withers from lack of use, she thought, the ability to chitchat—an inevitable atrophy that comes from the many hours she spent alone now, and the loss of that easy daily companionship with Torre. She used to share all that had gone on during her day, telling him bits of news large and small, a steady trickle of conversation that now was dammed up but that, oddly, did not seem to pour forth as one might expect when she was around others.

While she was opening kitchen cupboard doors to find containers for leftovers, the front door opened again.

In the fading evening light stood a young auburn-haired woman in a long-sleeved T-shirt and a fluid short skirt.

Esme.

"Gardenia, nice to see you." Esme leaned forward to offer a gentle hug.

"It's been such a long time. Medical school is treating you OK?" Gardenia asked. "Are you still thinking about neurosurgery?"

"Yep. 'A glutton for punishment,' as my grandma would say. How is Hans? I hear he's married and has a baby."

"Milo. Almost nineteen months now. The cutest child on the planet." She handed Esme the one unclaimed piece of cake.

"It must take a lot of time, being a dad to a toddler. But I know he'll get back to his music. He is such an awesome pianist." Esme excised bits of chocolate ganache with the precision of someone who would one day slice into human brains.

"Life is long," Gardenia suggested. No way was she going to reveal that she worried that Hans had lost his chance at a brilliant career as a pianist because of Milo's birth. He would never catch up with Jacob Newsome-Jones. The world of music was brutal.

Esme meticulously rinsed her cake plate. "Good to see you. I'm going to say hi to my parents and my granny."

Gardenia scraped the last of the plates and loaded the dishwasher before saying good-bye to Sylvie and Doug.

"So soon?" Sylvie said. "People will be hanging around for a while."

"I'm beat. But thanks for inviting me."

Bruce gave her a paper napkin with his scrawled phone number and asked for hers. "Gardenia, it was great to meet you. You can call me anytime you want to talk about him. Think about the taking turns idea, OK?"

"Maybe," she said. "And by the way, *him* is Torre."

"Sure. Torre. And my wife is Janine."

"I know, you told me. And my husband was Torre," she repeated.

As she hurried down the front porch steps to her car, she said softly to herself: *Torre. Torre. Torre.*

Yes, it did feel good to say his name.

Chapter Fourteen

"That young lady, Frieda, is a nice sort, to offer us tickets," Dorothy Wiggens said to her son as she gripped his arm and stepped carefully across the parking lot to the Lakeshore Theatre by Green Lake. "How old is she?"

"One never asks, but I'd wager she's crested the four-decade mark," Arnold said.

"See, only forty. That's when life begins. Well, for some, anyway." Dorothy stopped to yank a patterned silk scarf into a tight knot around her neck, to keep it from slipping but also, it seemed, to emphasize the fact that life begins at forty and, by extension, that forty-eight-year-old Arnold had some catching up to do.

Frieda, waving from the theater entrance, looked like some miniature breed of creature chosen for its springy hair and tiny hooflike feet.

Arnold wished her face had not lit up when he greeted her.

He wished that his mother had not seen that lit-up face.

"It's a good thing I got tickets in advance," Frieda said as she hugged Dorothy. Arnold stepped back to put some space between himself and Frieda and thus thwart a hug. "This isn't the biggest theater in town, but when they do a good play, people find out."

"It was kind of you to invite us, dear," Dorothy said. "Arnold and I used to come to this theater years ago. We even bought subscriptions, didn't we, honey?"

"I'm happy to treat you both," Frieda said, spreading her hands in a gesture as if inviting them to a banquet table. "But, Arn, that doesn't mean you're off the hook. Next time *you* can invite *me*." She swatted his arm with her rolled-up program.

"Seems the Lakeshore has soldiered on without us," Arnold said, coaxing the conversation back to his mother's remark.

The audience sat on three sides of the stage, which was simply a wide expanse of floor tricked out, for this production, with a chintz-covered sofa, some easy chairs, and a dining room table. The play was a comedy by a British playwright and would have crisp dialogue, wry humor, and eccentric characters.

Arnold wondered what such a writer would do with Chaucer's work. He had seen a stage version of *The Canterbury Tales*, but it had not begun to convey the richness of the original. A master makes it look so easy, he thought, but just attempt something similar, and one discovers quickly how difficult it is to improve on genius. And how many authors—even accomplished ones—could pull off an extended tale in rhyme?

"The F-word, dear," Dorothy was saying to Frieda as the last patrons took their seats. "I hope this is not one of those plays where they say it over and over. As if that's funny, saying bad words."

"The students who do the poetry slam, it's all about 'Fuck this' and 'Shit that,'" Frieda declared. "But I don't complain. No, I don't. Even though to me that is *not* poetry. You never know when one of those so-called poets might consider taking one of my classes and bringing some friends along. Got to keep the seats filled, right, Arn?"

"Satisfying the Youth of Today," Arnold mumbled into his program. Frieda didn't understand that class enrollment was a touchy subject, like alluding to one's attempts to lose weight or save money. Or find a suitable publisher. Frieda might know that he was being demoted, despite what Dodge had said about not telling anyone else. And if Frieda knew, Laurel might.

Horses were out of barns and cats out of bags, but if he got a yes for his manuscript from Yale soon, maybe Dodge would change his mind. An impending publication would raise his status among students, who would rush to enroll in his classes.

Arnold would ask Laurel soon about mentioning his manuscript to her editor. Yale's delay in following up on his query didn't mean that his book was lacking. It simply signaled the volume of manuscripts that the best academic presses received and the challenge of getting one's work to rise to the top of the slush pile.

The theater's artistic director strode onstage and made the usual sincere comments about the production: The cast was a joy to work with, the tech crew was skilled and professional, and the new season of plays was amazing, should anyone want to subscribe.

"Shall we three subscribe together?" Frieda whispered to Arnold.

The elderly woman in front of them saved him from replying when she turned around and glared at Frieda with a sharp "Shhh!"

Arnold himself breached theater etiquette the next moment as he gasped loudly.

Laurel had slithered into the theater, her pale hair beaconing her arrival in the dark. She took one of the last seats available, in the back of the bank at stage right, so that Arnold, in his seat at the back of the center section, could watch her as easily as he could the actors.

Too distracted to join in the appreciative laughter of those around him as the cast ably declaimed the play's British witticisms, Arnold instead plotted his strategy for intermission.

My fine fellow, he told himself, you need do nothing but greet Laurel politely and introduce Dorothy. Let the two of them decide the direction of the conversation and what your role in it may be, if any. It will be easy enough to insert an explanation along the lines of "Frieda kindly offered Mother an extra ticket, and one for me as well." He would mention that he was responsible for driving his mother to the theater so Laurel would not necessarily assume that he and Frieda were on a date. Still, he hoped that by some miracle Laurel would not see them in the small theater or the lobby.

"I'm off to the restroom," Frieda said at intermission.

"I shall use the loo as well," Dorothy said, as if infected by proximity to British slang.

"I'll stay here," Arnold said, but Dorothy either did not hear him or chose not to, as she held her hand out to him for assistance.

Across the theater Laurel was intent on reading her program. Perhaps he would be able to manage escorting his mother to the restroom door without being seen. If the three of them stayed in their seats long enough when the play ended, they might not encounter Laurel outside the theater. Ah, the vagaries of romantic attraction! It was possible to fantasize about the beloved throughout the day but, when sharing the same patch of real estate after hours, to want only to avoid meeting face-to-face.

"I thought that was you, sitting there with your mother and Hamm."

Laurel whacked Arnold's arm with her rolled-up program as he waited for his mother by the lobby espresso cart.

"Ah, and I was sure that was our po-mo specialist creeping in as the theater lights went down."

"One of my students is the stage manager and gave me a free ticket. Haven't been to this theater before, but I have to say, they're doing an OK job. So you and Frieda take your mother along when you go out? The dutiful son and all that?"

"Frieda bought two extra tickets that she offered to my mother and me, since I am my mother's chauffeur," Arnold said, using the lines he had scripted for himself. "And I do appreciate British wit."

"I get most of the jokes. At least I *think* I do. You would be the one to understand what they think is funny, though. The Anglophile."

"Indeed."

Dorothy had tottered over to them.

"Thank you for waiting, dear. And who is this?"

"Dr. Laurel DuBarr, our new post-modern literature professor. Dr. DuBarr, this is my mother, Dorothy Wiggens."

"Oh, enough with all that 'Dr. DuBarr' stuff, Arn."

"People think he's a medical doctor when I call him *Dr.* Wiggens," Dorothy said. "You know, a lot of people don't realize that there are all sorts of ways to be a doctor."

Arnold said, "Laurel is an expert in post-modern literary criticism."

"I'm sure I'm ancient and set in my ways and don't understand what that means," Dorothy said. "I always like a good mystery. Some of the new books I pick up at the library, I can't read past the first page."

"Laurel, what are you doing here?" Frieda wiped some droplets of water from her cheek, the result of a spray from the drinking fountain.

"Seeing the play."

"A coincidence, that all three of us—I mean *four*—would end up here on the same night."

A bell signaled the end of the intermission. Arnold offered Dorothy his arm while Frieda and Laurel entered the theater together, the miniature breed and the high-strung racing filly.

The second act was surprisingly sprightly, though Dorothy's head lolled toward her chest as she napped through half of it. Arnold felt sad, as he always did, when he glimpsed his mother asleep. Her octogenarian face was wrinkled and colorless, her mouth hung open, and a thread of drool escaped down her chin.

When the audience began applauding appreciatively at the end, Dorothy woke up with a start and turned to Frieda.

"Oh fiddle, I must have missed the best part. I hope I didn't offend you, dear, since you offered me the ticket. I did enjoy what I saw. Not a single bad word."

"Never mind," Frieda said. "You were awake for the first act."

A few stray "fucks" and "shags" had crept into the second act while Dorothy was napping, though not spoken loudly enough to awake her.

"British wit was what the doctor ordered, you might say," Arnold said, and noting Frieda's quizzical look, he realized he wasn't sure exactly what he meant by this either.

"Let's do this again. Remember, your treat next time, Arn." The rolled-program slap landed on his shoulder this time.

"I'm sure Arnold will be happy to buy tickets for all of us next time. Won't you, honey?" Dorothy said.

"Ah," he said, not at all happy at the prospect of another evening with Frieda, who would use the occasion as proof that he *liked* her.

Laurel was at the edge of the stage chatting animatedly with a young dreadlocked woman—the student stage manager who had offered her the ticket? The two laughing together reminded Arnold of how long it had been since he'd had such a lively conversation with a student. He recalled that during his first years at the University of the Northwest, one eager lad or coed had often followed him from the classroom, determined to share his or her revelations about the Wife of Bath or "The Miller's Tale." Nowadays students rushed away, heads bent in obeisance to their smartphones. They accosted him only when they had grade issues or wanted to plead for an early final exam date so they could leave for a vacation in Hawaii.

Well, that didn't mean he wasn't a fine teacher. His low enrollments were due not to a lack of interest in his subject or dissatisfaction with his teaching style but instead to the inexorable tramp of technology through the hallowed halls of academe. And no conversation with a real human being could compete with the siren call of the iPhone between classes.

At least he was on his way to adding PowerPoint to his lectures, thanks to Laurel's help. During their walk at Magnuson Park, she had first talked at some length about her running regimen and a case of tendonitis she had suffered the previous year, and after that, she discussed—well, complained about—the various community colleges that had hired her as an adjunct.

Finally she had pulled her tired-looking PowerPoint manual from her bag and offered it to him with a flourish, saying "No reason for me to waste my time telling you what you can learn by reading this. I assume you've got your visuals downloaded?"

To this he had answered something noncommittal. He would need hours and hours to assemble images related to Chaucer's world.

Wait. You won't be teaching Chaucer much longer anyway, he had reminded himself. One could call that a silver lining, no need to learn PowerPoint, except that it also eliminated the need for Laurel's advice and thus, time alone with her.

"I'd like to invite those nice young ladies to brunch," Dorothy said as she climbed into the Volvo's passenger seat. "Frieda and I get on like a house afire. I'll invite the other gal, just for the fun of female company. You are invited. If both of them come, it won't look like I'm matchmaking, will it?"

"Frankly, Mumsie, I do not know." Arnold hoped the idea would slip her mind.

Chapter Fifteen

"Hey, Mom, any chance you could watch Milo tonight? They offered me some overtime, but Caitlin made a plan to meet up with some old high school friends."

"Well, sure," Gardenia said, switching her cell to speakerphone so she could finish folding a stack of tea towels while she took Hans's call. "But I'm not sure I want to be out late. I have to be at work by eight thirty tomorrow."

"Caitlin should be home by ten. Can you be over by seven thirty? I have to leave around six but Caitlin can wait until then."

Into her backpack Gardenia slipped a Barbara Pym novel, *Jane and Prudence*, which she'd started to read the week before. The rhythms of life in provincial postwar Britain soothed her—the lumbering pace of the characters' days, their cumbersome means of communication, the letters and postcards and waiting for a phone call, and Pym's wry recording of all this. I feel less dull when I consider the lives of Pym's people, she thought, or is it that I identify with their dullness? Never mind, this was the kind of escape she needed.

She didn't dare count on anything worthwhile in the young

couple's bookcase, with Caitlin's lurid-covered paperback romances jammed next to Hans's carefully organized volumes of sheet music.

Gardenia knocked on the townhouse door promptly at seven thirty.

"Say hi to your grandma." Caitlin held Milo out to Gardenia as if he were slightly radioactive. "It's been one of those days. He tipped an entire bowl of peas on the kitchen floor, and the top came off his sippy cup. Man, do I need a break."

"Hey there, precious." Gardenia held Milo close. Hans had had a hard day, but did *he* get to go out with friends tonight? she thought. No indeed, he was working an extra shift to help pay for diapers and peas and sippy cups and his wife's evenings out with her friends.

"Mimaw," Milo said, cozying into Gardenia's embrace.

"Does he always call me that, *Mimaw*?"

"What? Oh, Hans trained him to say that. Don't know why. Milo calls my mom *Mommalee*. That's cute."

"Mimaw loves you," Gardenia said rather loudly. Whatever Hans and Milo want to call me is fine, she thought, and *Mimaw* is as cute as *Mommalee*.

Cuter.

Milo clung to her like a baby chimp. Babies were such little *mammals*, when it came right down to it, responding to those who kept their stomachs full and who held them in a close, protective embrace. Oh, she loved this tiny boy! She wanted to spend every possible minute with him, even if she was aiding and abetting selfish behavior in Caitlin.

"Um, I'm not sure Hans mentioned this, but if you could spend the night, that would be great. I think we girls are going to be out pretty late. They want to go to a movie and out for drinks afterward. Jen's birthday and all that. I'll stay over at her place. Not sure when Hans will be home—we didn't talk at all today. I think he has to clean up the store and help with inventory."

"But I didn't bring my toothbrush or pajamas."

"There's a new toothbrush in the top drawer of the vanity. Hey, you can wear the nightgown that Mommalee left when she stayed over last week."

"All right, but I'll have to get up early and go home, to get ready for work."

"Sure. Must feel good to be earning something. Hans was worried that you didn't have enough, but I said you must have some insurance money."

Fortunately, focusing on holding Milo in her arms made it easier for Gardenia not to snap back at this remark.

Caitlin applied some lip gloss deftly, without looking in a mirror. The hem of her purply-pink silk blouse didn't cover the ripple of skin above the front of her low-slung jeans.

"Amazing to me that you and your friends can stay out so late," Gardenia ventured. "Seems I wanted to sleep more than anything else when Hans was Milo's age."

"The way I see it, take care of yourself and you can be a better mother. Anyway, I'm late. Bye-bye, pumpkin." She kissed the top of Milo's head.

The baby's lower lip trembled as Caitlin opened the front door.

"What movie are you going to? And maybe I should have the name of the bar?" Gardenia called to Caitlin.

"Text me if you've got a problem. Or Hans." Caitlin paused to pull a perfume atomizer from her bag to spritz herself. "Really, I'm *so* late."

Gardenia held Milo up to the front window and pumped his

chubby arm up and down in a wave good-bye as Caitlin strode out of sight. Tears rolled down his cheeks. Whoever was picking up Caitlin must have been waiting down the street.

"Mama will be back, Mama will be back, and here's Mimaw to take care of you, my precious." She launched into the first verse of "Froggie Went A-Courtin'," the folk song she often used to distract him, while she changed his diaper and put on his yellow sleeper.

As she gave Milo his bottle and rocked him to sleep, she reminded herself of her good luck. I live close to my only grandchild, she told herself, I'm invited to take care of him, and I can see my only child every week. But these blessings don't change the fact that I've been sensing for weeks now that all is not well between Hans and Caitlin.

The couple hadn't talked at all that day, yet Torre had always called her at least once when she was home with baby Hans, to see how things were going and if he could pick up anything from the store on his way home.

And Caitlin was going to spend the night elsewhere again.

Dollars to doughnuts she's not out with the "girls," Gardenia thought, but with some other guy. The rage she felt at this thought made her rock so vigorously that Milo's eyes popped open, but he quickly fell back to sleep.

Tall, buxom Mommalee's left-behind flannel nightgown, with its pattern of holly sprigs and laughing snowmen, billowed around Gardenia. Caitlin's mother shared her daughter's penchant for perfume, and Aroma of Mommalee so impregnated the gown that Gardenia decided to sleep in her clothes instead, as uncomfortable as she knew that might be.

But no. She pictured Caitlin harping to Hans about how finicky his mother is.

Listen, you have to stay on Caitlin's good side, Gardenia lectured herself. Take the high road and all that. If you don't, Caitlin can decide that you're not fit to take care of Milo. And she has her own mother to be the one-and-only granny if you fall out of favor.

Gardenia slipped out of her jeans and turtleneck, pulled the cloyingly fragrant gown down over her head, settled on the sofa with a pillow from the linen closet and a fleece blanket, and read only two Pym chapters before falling asleep.

~

"You were out with *girlfriends*? Ha! You're lying to me and to my son. You are such a princess, you take advantage of your mother-in-law as a babysitter so you can go out and spend the night with another man. Your husband, my wonderful Hans, is working day and night, literally, to keep up his end of the bargain, and you cheat on him? Don't think I won't advise Hans to file for divorce tomorrow. He'll get custody of Milo, and I'll take care of my grandson. You'll be free to run around as you please, but don't come crying to me when you get tired of that other man and want your family back."

The unspoken words pounded in Gardenia's brain as a rumpled Caitlin walked, yawning, in the door at six thirty in the morning.

What Gardenia said instead was: "I put your mother's nightgown in the laundry hamper."

"Thanks. Milo's not up?"

"No, but I set the alarm on my phone so I'd be up by six and ready for him."

"Hey, you could have slept in. Hans usually gets up with him."

"He got home late, Caitlin." Gardenia half awoke when she'd heard Hans creep in, but she didn't say anything to him and instead pretended to be asleep on the sofa. He had uncorked the bottle of white jug wine that she'd seen in the fridge and poured and poured into something larger than a wineglass. The floorboards of the bedroom had murmured as he tiptoed in to check on Milo. Later came the sounds of soft tapping on the laptop keyboard and the intermittent picking up and setting down of the vessel he had chosen for his generous pour of wine.

Milo had not stirred all night, although Gardenia found she had slept fitfully on the soft sofa, hyperalert to any whimpering from the crib.

"It's a miracle I was able to get home this early. I would have slept until noon if I hadn't set my phone alarm," Caitlin said.

Wise woman that she hoped she was, Gardenia said nothing as she put on her jacket, shouldered her backpack, and peeked at the softly snoring Milo.

"I hope he stays asleep for a while," Caitlin whispered as Gardenia emerged from the bedroom. "I wouldn't mind crawling back into bed myself. Hans can get up with him so I can sleep some."

At this Gardenia whisked herself out the door, which was the only way she could ensure that she would not growl some words she'd later regret.

The milky-gray haze of the early-morning sky showed tiny slivers of blue that meant the cloudiness would burn off and that the day would be brilliant and sunny by late morning. The azaleas around the neighborhood were in bloom, the blossoms on the rhododendrons ready to pop open. In the distance the Olympics seemed deceptively near, as if one could paddle a kayak across the Sound to reach them. A perfect late April day ahead, Gardenia thought, but she wished instead that it would start to pour down cold rain so she could call in sick, light a fire in the fireplace, and huddle on the couch all day with Susie, letting herself make waste of an entire box of tissues while she blubbered.

"Torre, Torre, I need you!" she yelled in the privacy of her Subaru.

"Don't jump to conclusions. You have no evidence that she's carrying on." Yes, this was what Torre would say. Gardenia could hear herself insisting that it was her duty as a mother to warn Hans of danger, even though he was an adult who was no longer hers to protect. And Torre would respond, "It's just what you *assume*. Not our business anyway."

Susie was whining at the front door when Gardenia walked in. Guiltily she picked up the little dog and rushed her out to the small patch of lawn.

"Sorry, sweetheart, you had to go so bad." In a plea for forgiveness, Gardenia drained the oil from a can of sardines onto Susie's kibble and mixed in two of the small fish for her. She remembered that she'd splurged on a box of frozen apricot Danish, in case Hans dropped by and wanted something to eat with a cup of tea. Now she put one of the pastries in the oven, made a fresh carafe of coffee, and poured three whisked eggs into a pool of melted butter, adding a handful of cheddar when they were set.

A robust, high-fat breakfast would soothe the pain of suspecting that her son's wife was a cheat and a liar.

Chapter Sixteen

ON THE FIRST Saturday in May Arnold wiped down the aged aluminum-and-nylon-webbing chaise lounge that he had inherited from his mother and stretched out on it on the back deck of his second-floor apartment, the remodeled upstairs of an older Capitol Hill home. Beside him on a molded plastic lawn chair was the slim stack of short-answer tests he had given to his students the previous day. He would grade them after enjoying his breakfast of fried eggs, sausage, toast, and his cuppa.

Usually Arnold was a sound sleeper, but the night before he had lain awake from 2:00 to 4:00 a.m., the thought of his demotion buzzing in his head like a swarm of tropical mosquitoes. Well, *demotion* might not be the correct word, Arnold comforted himself. He would maintain his tenure and his position as a senior faculty member. But the thought of losing his Chaucer and Middle English courses and being subjected to training undergrads to create cogent paragraphs made him want to ululate with frustration.

All the more reason to forge ahead with trying to get his book published.

As he lounged on the upstairs deck, Arnold had a view, across the alley, of the small gilded onion domes of the Saint Nicholas Russian Orthodox Cathedral. How odd, Arnold thought, that a resolutely unreligious person such as I would live in a neighborhood crammed with churches. Two blocks west, facing Cal Anderson Park, was a petite Lutheran church, its brick construction and dimensions suggesting that it had escaped from a quaint English village. A block away was the enigmatic German United Church of Christ, its humble bilingual signboard stating that all services were conducted in German, though it was hard to imagine that there were enough native-German speakers in Seattle to fill even one pew.

When he walked to work with Leroy down 14th Avenue, they passed the First AME Church and the Progressive Missionary Baptist Church, its belfry windows covered with plywood and yellowed drapes hanging in the windows of what must have been a basement fellowship room. And sharing the same block with Saint Nicholas was a grand brick building with a square turret and boarded-up windows, *First Advent Christian Church* inscribed on the concrete cornerstone. Now it was used by a group of Ethiopian evangelists.

Sundays at this section of Capitol Hill must have once meant sidewalks full of behatted and shiny-shoed parishioners, Arnold thought. Now you would hardly know a Saturday from a Sunday from a Tuesday, the apartment dwellers no longer churchgoers but instead spending their weekends shopping or googling or watching movies on giant flat-screened TVs.

"You might try a church." So Dorothy had suggested once when the topic of his bachelorhood had again surfaced in their conversation. "Ann Landers always said church was the best place to meet someone. Not a bar. You won't find a petunia in an onion patch."

"What do you think, my friend?" Arnold asked Leroy. "Do Russian

Orthodox men seek petunias under those onion domes?" He set his breakfast plate in front of the dachshund, who desperately gobbled the last bites of sausage and a scrap of toast and the crispy fringe from a fried egg. Sipping the last of his Keemun, Arnold settled back into the chaise and admired the neighbor's magnolia with its fat—might one even say *pregnant*?—buds, next in line to blossom as the leisurely Seattle spring unfolded.

Just this moment, Arnold thought. Just this *now*. A Zen concept, and one far more suited to my religious philosophy than some claptrap about a zealot Jewish boy and his sad death nailed to a cross. Why do I need anything more than just this, despite my mother's conviction that a "normal life" with a family is the only way to find fulfillment?

Yet even as he reassured himself, an image of himself with Laurel, the two of them strolling past Saint Nicholas Russian Orthodox Cathedral, came to mind.

This time the image included himself with a baby strapped to his front.

"You up there?" Harry, Arnold's new downstairs neighbor, called from the weedy patch of lawn that was their shared backyard.

"Yes, so it seems."

"The wife asked me to have a little chat with you."

"Oh?"

"About your dog. Can I come up?"

"Yes, you *may*," Arnold said. I hope this little chat will be quick, he thought, as I have papers to grade. And a bask in the sunshine to complete.

Encouraged by the warm morning, Harry wore a pair of skimpy denim shorts and an open-necked short-sleeved shirt, a gold chain lying on his hairy chest. He held a cigarette between the stained index and second finger of his left hand. Arnold stood up when Harry reached the top of the stairs leading to the deck, but he did not move the stack of tests off the lawn chair and invite him to sit. Leroy backed up and began to bark sharply.

"See? That's it," Harry said. "He barks all the time. Morning, noon, and night. We understand that when you are sharing a house with somebody, you're gonna have some noise. Give and take, you know. But not a dog barking all day long."

"That's enough, good sir," Arnold said, and clamped his hand gently on Leroy's muzzle. "He couldn't be barking all day long. I take him to work with me."

"Well, OK. Maybe the wife is exaggerating some." Harry pulled on his skinny white ponytail—he had announced to Arnold at their first meeting, as if to answer inevitable questions, that he had retired from a lifelong career as an insurance salesman and had resolved never again to get a business haircut or wear a suit and tie.

"And he doesn't bark when I'm home with him," Arnold said as he crouched down to reassure the now-silent Leroy.

"It must be when you're gone and he's not with you. Doesn't like to be alone. I had a dog like that once. We had to give him away. A nuisance. Anyway, just so you know. A warning." Harry looked around for a place to stub out his cigarette and chose the edge of a terra-cotta pot that Arnold filled with red geraniums each summer.

"*Warning?*"

"I mean, I may have to tell the landlord. Our lease says no pets, by the way."

"That's not what my lease says." Arnold placed himself at the top of the wooden staircase, wishing he had a door to open to more clearly signal that it was time for Harry to leave. He had been a loyal and responsible tenant for five years. The previous downstairs renter had never said anything about Leroy's barking, albeit she was a frenetically busy young woman who slammed the front door at eight on weekday mornings and opened it again at ten at night. She wasn't around during those occasional hours when Leroy was alone and might have been vocalizing. Or maybe the dachshund had only recently developed this habit?

"At least I wanted you to know. Didn't want you to get an eviction notice someday and wonder why."

Harry picked his way down the stairs, as if not used to his post-retirement huaraches, and crossed the yard to his apartment door at the front of the house.

"Asshole!" This was the one swear word that sparked in Arnold's mind when he had to deal with someone like Harry. Although he had no intention of being anything but a cordial neighbor, he would not abide accusations that made Leroy guilty until proven innocent. He would speak with the landlord directly.

The pleasant morning he had been enjoying, with the prospect of leisurely hours for grading papers and also working on his book, was now marred by Harry's entrance onto the stage. He still had the rest of Saturday and Sunday to "buckle down," as his mother would say. Today he would declare for himself the holiday he deserved. Besides, he wanted to find out forthwith if Harry's allegations were true by leaving Leroy alone in the apartment for a few hours.

In a small black shoulder bag that he had found at a garage sale he packed his swim trunks, goggles, and a towel.

Arnold coated the inside of a rubber Kong toy with peanut butter, using a small knife he kept for the purpose, and tossed it into Leroy's bed just as he left.

"Now, my friend, this is an excellent chance for a siesta. I'm off for a swim, and the sad truth is that dachshunds aren't allowed."

Arnold chose to walk the many blocks to the public pool for his weekly swim rather than drive or wait for a bus. He could have chosen to go to the UNW pool, but he had decided when he was hired not to swim there and risk running into students and other faculty members, in various stages of disrobing, in the locker room.

Ahead of him was a young couple, the man wearing cutoffs that revealed an elaborate tattoo of Elvis on his right calf. A tattooed image of a flame crawled up the back of his neck. The young woman had tousled pink hair, her bare upper arms festooned with tattoos of some Asian pictographs.

Arnold did not realize until he passed the pair that a baby was riding in a front-facing carrier pack on the young man's chest. The baby's white-blond hair gleamed in the late-morning sun. Arnold wondered for a moment if the baby might be tattooed, but he—or she—wasn't. The child's chubby arms pumped up and down with the rhythm of the father's stride. The mother leaned over and kissed the child's cheek, grabbed her partner's arm to stop him for a second, and kissed his cheek.

The baby turned and grinned at Arnold.

Arnold strode quickly past the little family, as if to distance himself from the source of an unexpected flare of envy. For years he had heard of one acquaintance or another becoming a parent. For years he had heard reports from his mother about the children of his former neighborhood friends and classmates. Never had he felt particularly wistful about the parenthood of others, not even (or especially?) when he had been with Maggie and starting a family had been a possibility. When he compared his own freedom with the responsibility of being a father, there was no contest.

And there were enough people—too many—on the planet, so why was the continuation of his DNA necessary?

And yet.

"I want a baby," Arnold said softly.

Never had he said these words to himself, much less aloud.

"I want a baby. I want a child," he said. Was this impulse the natural sap rising brought on by an exceptionally warm and fragrant May morning? Was it the fetching smile of that toothless, round-faced baby? Was it the contrast between the baby and his parents, the force of nature not minding who made another human being? If this couple, seemingly harmonious despite their latter-day punk appearance, could enjoy a baby, why couldn't—or shouldn't—Arnold Wiggens?

"This too shall pass," Arnold told himself, hearing his mother's voice, though she would be appalled to think it was being applied to her son's sudden urge to make her a grandmother.

At the pool he changed into his swim trunks in one of the toilet stalls in the men's dressing room, showered, and slipped into the slow lap lane of the pool. Once in the cold water, acrid with chlorine, he forced himself to think about something besides babies while he swam an easy sidestroke. His book, for example. This was his *real* baby, the progeny of his heart and mind. Anyone could copulate for a few minutes and become a parent, yet few human beings had the intelligence and perception to pay homage to the great Geoffrey Chaucer through exquisitely rendered literary analysis.

But the issue of fatherhood was his inescapable torment for the day. Babies and small children appeared everywhere, as if a soft rain had fallen overnight and coaxed them into bloom.

A dozen small children in bathing suits filed into the pool area. Their mothers, also in swimsuits, guided the little ones to sit on a bench while they waited for the adult lap swim to end and swimming lessons to begin. One little boy began to cry, saying that he didn't want to get into the water, and his mother crouched beside him and said something in a sharp tone that Arnold was sure he would never use with a—*his?*—fearful child.

While heading home after his swim, Arnold stopped to buy some groceries. In a cart at the checkout sat a small girl with two stick-out pigtails. A dark-eyed little boy was perched in the cart behind. He held the door open for a woman with a toddler in a stroller and a baby in a sling. A father wrestled a crying infant out of a car a block from his apartment.

Calm down, old man, Arnold told himself. The universe is playing a little joke: Guess what? There are so many sweet babies in the world, but not one is yours, because that's the way you wanted it, *n'est-ce pas?*

From the half-open window of his apartment that faced the street came a wail.

A baby?

No, it was Leroy, punctuating his desperate whining with sharp barks.

"Back just in time for the performance." Harry leaned over the porch railing, puffing his cigarette. "Don't tell me you can't hear *that*. The wife couldn't settle in for her afternoon nap because of all the yapping."

Arnold felt as he had as an eight-year-old when a bully cornered him on the playground and shook him down for his homemade chocolate chip cookies. But perhaps because he heard Arnold's voice, Leroy had stopped barking.

"Do you hear him now?" Arnold stood straighter.

"It'll start up again in a minute, just wait," Harry said.

Leroy—bless him—didn't make a sound.

"What if Leroy were a baby crying away in the upstairs apartment? Would you demand that I sedate or evict him?" Arnold asked.

"A baby, now that's a different story. The wife always has a soft spot for babies. Guess because we never had one ourselves." At this Harry looked back toward the downstairs apartment that held his napless, childless wife, his shoulders slumping an inch. "Have a good one," Harry called, waving from the porch as Arnold unlocked the front door leading to the second-floor staircase.

Leroy greeted him with his usual ecstatic tail wagging and began to warble with pleasure. Arnold picked him up.

"If it comes to that, we will find another home together, noble sir," Arnold said. "In the meantime, we'll work on making you the strong, silent type."

Chapter Seventeen

Gardenia could not help noticing, as she and Sylvie began their Sunday-morning stride around Green Lake, that her friend wore brand-new sneakers, in trendy bright green and yellow, while she plodded along in her old white walking shoes, dingy from the many hours they had spent in the garden.

Silly of me to care, Gardenia thought. I'm not a middle-school girl who sizes up her friends by the shoes they wear. Still, she could never have afforded such expensive shoes. Her windbreaker was frumpy compared with Sylvie's lightweight raspberry-colored jacket.

As if reading her mind, the kind Sylvie said, "You always look so pretty, even when we're dressed down—I mean, *casually*—to go for a walk."

"Really? I was just thinking how old-fashioned my shoes are, compared to yours."

"Oh please. As if anyone cares. I wouldn't have new things if Doug wasn't so interested in buying the latest gear. For some reason he wants me to keep up with him."

Torre never seemed to notice changes in fashion, Gardenia started to say, and he always told me I looked nice in whatever I was wearing, but Sylvie broke in: "Esme seems to have a beau."

"Nice! Who?" Yes, Gardenia thought, a *beau* is exactly what the dazzling Esme would have, not simply a *boyfriend* or *partner,* nothing as carnal as a *lover*.

"Someone she knows from med school. Another student, I guess, though she changed the subject when I asked more about him."

Sylvie shrugged, unzipped her jacket in the warm May sunshine, and turned away from Gardenia to watch a solo rower scull a slender racing shell. "Smell the air!" she said. "Lilacs blooming somewhere."

"I thought Esme usually told you about her social life?" Could it be that Sylvie and her perfect daughter might have "communication problems"?

"She's her own woman now," Sylvie said. "I'm learning to keep quiet."

"But aren't you curious? I mean, aren't you dying to know who it is?"

"Of course. But my relationship with Esme is more important. I don't want to pry. Hey, did I tell you that Doug is looking to change jobs?"

"I thought he liked that company."

"Just at the talk stage now. He says he's going to start seeing what else is out there."

"There's so much going on in Seattle now. And the Eastside? There must be *tons* of tech companies that would want him," Gardenia said.

"We'll see." Sylvie looked away.

Gardenia didn't ask her friend for more details because they were both distracted by the sight of a woman cloaked in a long brown gown and veil. With a curtain of matching fabric covering her face from the eyes down, she pushed a stroller toward them on the opposite side of the path. Like Sylvie, the woman wore brightly colored sneakers. Her eyes met Gardenia's as she passed. It was impossible to tell how old the woman might be.

"Here we are, trying not to pry into our children's lives, and that woman probably had to marry someone her parents chose for her," Gardenia said. "And her husband has the right to tell her to wear that awful burka thing, even on a beautiful day like this." Gardenia yanked off her windbreaker, as if to demonstrate that American women can take off and put on clothing as they wish.

"If it's what she likes to wear," Sylvie began, "and it is their culture . . ." But Gardenia interrupted.

"It's not a matter of *like*. What happens if she doesn't want to cover herself up? Does she have a choice? It's a human rights issue, not 'their culture.'" Gardenia almost added, *And what happens to a young Muslim wife if she becomes interested in another man?*

"Wow, didn't expect that." Sylvie put her arm around Gardenia's shoulders. "You're right. We are lucky, to have been born when and where we were and to have so many choices."

Walking for several steps with her friend's arm around her, Gardenia felt herself slump with a mixture of longing and relief. How long it had been since Torre had put his arm around her! How long it had been since Hans had put his arm around her! Nowadays her closest body contact was with Susie and Milo.

"Speaking of babies," Sylvie said, "which was not exactly what we were speaking of, but seeing the stroller reminded me that I was going to ask for a Milo update."

Dear Sylvie knows this is the sure way to cheer me up, Gardenia thought. Sylvie listened to Gardenia's chatter about Milo and his newest words and the songs he liked Mimaw to sing and the way he jumped into her arms when she visited.

"Lucky you, as I've said many times," Sylvie said. "To have a grandchild when you're still so young. And to have him and Hans living nearby."

With the silence that their long friendship made perfectly comfortable, they passed the boathouse, where Gardenia and Hans had often rented a paddleboat in the summer, and the soccer field where Hans had run clumsily up and down with his grade-school team, the Ghostbusters. Hans had kicked maybe one successful goal in his entire soccer career, but Gardenia and Torre had gone to all the matches, bundled against the cold and rain while cheering with the other loyal parents.

Someday Milo might play soccer. He was almost certain to play soccer—all kids in Northeast Seattle seemed to be dragooned into soccer. She would faithfully attend Milo's games, the grandma at the sidelines that the young parents would politely greet but forget about as the game and their own conversations progressed.

Gardenia recalled the grandfather of one of Hans's teammates, who would sit in his wheelchair on the sidelines, a heavy plaid blanket pulled up to his chin. Had she ever said more than hello to this elder? Or offered to buy him a coffee from the booth near the boathouse? His family members had taken care of him, she reasoned, but she understood now how he must have felt, nearly invisible among the younger people and not of particular interest to them.

"How's Caitlin doing?" Sylvie asked. "Isn't she in school?"

"Yes, though she seems to have lots of time to hang out with her girlfriends."

"Ah," Sylvie said.

She held Gardenia's gaze for a second, as if to encourage her to spill, but Gardenia looked away. She wanted to share her suspicions of Caitlin, but she was ashamed, even though judgment-shy Sylvie would be understanding and reassuring.

A young couple jogged past, the woman holding the leash of a large black Lab and the father pushing a double stroller with infant twins. Behind them were parents with a long-legged girl, who hung on to her father's arm and said something that made him laugh. Two white-haired women, one tall and slim and the other short and stout, jabbered to each other in what Gardenia guessed was Russian. A teenage boy with a long ponytail, dyed green, shot past on a skateboard.

"Life, passing by us!" Gardenia exclaimed. "All these people with their own lives. And no one knows what's going to happen!"

"That's right," Sylvie said, blinking at this sudden declaration. "But anyway, it's good to be alive on a day like this, don't you think?"

"Not really," Gardenia said louder than was necessary for Sylvie to hear, as if she were delivering her one important line in an amateur melodrama. "Not really, when you think your only son has a cheating wife."

As soon as she had spoken these words, Gardenia scolded herself for betraying Hans by gossiping about his marriage.

"What? I thought you said Hans is crazy about Caitlin."

"He may be, but I'm not so sure what she's up to. She stays the night with girlfriends. We never stayed the night with girlfriends when our kids were little, did we?"

"No."

"Something about her, I just don't trust," Gardenia said. "Though I guess I feel sorry for her. I was going through a stack of their magazines and found this paper she wrote for a course last quarter. It was like something a middle schooler would write. Maybe she has dyslexia or something."

"She's brave to be back in school, trying to get a degree," Sylvie said.

Which was true, but Gardenia was not ready to lavish excessive compassion on Caitlin.

Mother bears do not lavish excessive compassion.

"I have to say, you have always been negative about Caitlin," Sylvie said.

"She's not the person I would have chosen for Hans. Not into music at all. What do they have in common?" Gardenia said as they approached their cars in the parking lot.

"Milo," Sylvie said. "And just wondering—when was the last time you all did something together?"

Her friend suggested, calmly and wisely, that Gardenia spend more time with the little family doing something fun. If Gardenia could see Caitlin and Hans in action as a couple—when they weren't handing Milo over to her before rushing out of the house—maybe she would understand the relationship better.

Back at home Gardenia texted Hans, asking if he and Milo and Caitlin would like to join her for an outing to Pike Place Market sometime.

A half hour later he texted back, "Can do next Sunday. Mother's Day!"

Chapter Eighteen

"Why do they always call it Pike's Market?" Gardenia asked as she and Hans left the middle-aged tourists who had just stopped them for directions.

"What?" Hans had politely waited with his mother while she pointed the couple toward Pike Place Market. Caitlin had crossed the street and resolutely pushed the stroller into the clot of pedestrians on the sidewalk.

"Tourists. They always call it Pike's Market. That summer two of Dad's friends from high school visited? They both called it that. I kept saying 'Pike Place Market,' but they didn't catch on." Gardenia was surprised to hear herself rant about this silly detail, like some cranky middle-aged character in a comedy. Maybe I'm keyed up because of this outing, she thought, excited about the fun of being with my son and grandson but wondering what I'm going to learn about Hans and Caitlin. "Oh well, what does it matter?" she said.

"Exactly. It doesn't matter, Mom. Maybe they all read the same guidebook and there was a typo or something."

Hans hurried ahead and caught up with his wife and son, leaving

Gardenia alone to navigate the shoals of visitors on this spring Sunday. She had set aside thirty dollars to treat them all to a lunch of fish and chips. She would order just a cup of chowder for herself. It was possible that Hans would offer to spring for lunch, though she would never suggest that he pay. Better that he use his hard-won cash on something else, maybe a little treat for himself. It must have been ages since he'd gone to a jazz club to hear some live music.

Hans put his arm around Caitlin's waist, but she pulled away and let him push the stroller. The day was edging to the midsixties, with a mosaic sky of pale gray clouds and patches of bright blue.

Hans stopped and turned to wave at Gardenia.

That's my boy, she thought with a rush of pride, and waved back. He's waiting for me—he loves his mama and will always look out for me.

Milo had dozed off in the stroller despite the noise and crowds.

Hans pulled the fleece blanket off Milo and patted his cheek.

"Just let him sleep," Caitlin said.

"But I want him to see the buskers. I used to love those guys playing music on the street. Hey, buddy, don't you want to wake up?"

The next fifteen minutes played out as Gardenia would have predicted.

Milo did open his eyes but immediately closed them again to recapture what must have been a deep sleep and happy dreams.

Hans lifted him out of the stroller.

Milo began to wail.

"I told you to leave him be!" Caitlin snapped at Hans.

"There are some buskers over there by Starbucks," Gardenia said as Hans tried to hoist Milo onto his shoulders to distract him from crying.

Caitlin declared she would meet up with them after she got a bag of minidoughnuts.

Hans pushed the stroller through the covered part of the Market, with its Hmong families selling the last of the season's tulips from their farms in the Skagit Valley. He stopped and bought two bunches. When Caitlin joined them with the small white bag of warm doughnuts, Hans thrust one bunch at her and one at Gardenia.

"Happy Mother's Day! From Milo and me."

"Hey, thanks," Caitlin said, and kissed him quickly on the cheek.

See what a considerate guy he is, Caitlin? Gardenia wanted to say. *Do you realize what an excellent husband and father he is?*

Hans parked the stroller in front of a group of buskers by the Starbucks store, one of the first and so a tourist attraction, visitors lining up to go inside.

"Did you come down to the Market when you were little?" Gardenia asked Caitlin.

"Once, when some friends of my parents were visiting. There's a video of me dancing and singing with somebody playing a guitar."

"I didn't know you like to sing. I think Milo is going to turn out to have a good voice. His grandpa Torre sure did," Gardenia said.

"Hans sings well." Caitlin finished another doughnut and put the rest in the carrier bag on the stroller. "Once my mom took me to a caroling party when I was about seven or eight. She told me to just mouth the words so I wouldn't ruin the sound."

"Maybe you had a cold or something?"

"No, she meant that I sounded terrible. So I haven't been into singing much." Caitlin joined Hans and Milo by the street performers.

Sylvie had been right, as usual. It was only a half hour into this outing, and already Gardenia had learned something about Caitlin that she hadn't known: Roxy Curlew was a thoughtless mother who told her daughter that she would "ruin the sound" if she sang along with Christmas carols.

In front of the Starbucks a young woman about Hans's age, in a short scarlet dress and beat-up cordovan oxfords, no socks, was plunking on a washtub bass to back up a banjo player and fiddler.

Milo bounced up and down in front of the musicians, just as toddler Hans had done with buskers.

"Now, you don't go nowhere, just stand here," said a man in a grimy sleeveless T-shirt to a little boy about three years old. The child had a shaved head, and he too wore a grimy sleeveless T-shirt and jeans.

The man—the boy's father?—lit a cigarette and jammed a pacifier back into the mouth of a cherubic blonde girl seated in a tattered stroller.

"Your mom's coming with something for you to eat. So you just stay put and I don't want to hear no crying," the man said to the silent boy.

"What lovely children," Gardenia said—would hearing this make the man kinder and gentler? "How old are they?"

"Let me think. This one is three. Three and a half?" He slapped the little boy's bald head. "And Miss Princess here, she's a year and a half."

Milo stared as the boy began to sway with the music.

"It's so fun for them to watch live music," Gardenia offered.

"I guess. We're just waiting for their mom to catch up. Jesus, what are all these people waiting for?"

"Tourists. It's one of the original Starbucks stores."

"That's just crazy." The man worked the stroller back and forth as the little girl began to whine. He hissed, "Keep it down!"

"I dancing." The little boy smiled at the man. Was this the child's father? Maybe just some boyfriend of his mom?

"Funniest looking dancing I ever saw," the man said.

"There you are!" The children's mother had a cigarette, a lip ring, and an exposed shoulder inked with tattoos. "Here's your lunch." She handed the boy a corn dog, which he ate as if famished, the music no longer holding his attention. When he was finished, he clung to his mother and mewled for another.

Dickensian, Gardenia thought as she jammed a dollar bill in the clear pitcher the buskers were using for a tip jar. To save herself the anguish of watching the sad little family any longer, she suggested to Hans that they find some fish and chips on the waterfront for lunch.

"Good idea," Hans said. "I'm starving."

"You could have had more doughnuts," Caitlin said.

"Naw, I need something solid."

Caitlin pushed the stroller while Hans carried Milo. Lounging on the benches at the edge of the park by the Market were homeless men, some with donation cups and scrawled signs declaring that they were veterans: *Anything helps*. A pod of affluent Chinese tourists were posing by the totem pole, while a large container ship chugged toward the port, perhaps laden with trinkets and cheap electronics made by their countrymen in crowded sweatshops.

Oh, it's all so confusing, random, and sad, Gardenia thought as she followed Hans and his family. Children born when and where they shouldn't be. Children who are adored by their parents, children who hear gruff commands and eat corn dogs. People harvesting tulips and pulling salmon out of the sea and designing T-shirts with images of Pike Place Market for the pleasure of people who have extra money to spend. All the babies here today will be gone in a hundred years. All the people my age will be gone in, max, forty-five years or so. Even the nubile young women pulling espresso will be gone in seventy or eighty years, maybe even less, and they will fray about the edges and get wrinkly and shriveled and maybe become widows, like me, before it is all over.

And each one of us will leave the world alone, no matter how much we have been loved, no matter how many happy years we've lived with and loved our family.

But no more worrying about Hans and Caitlin, Gardenia told herself. It could be so much worse—a daughter-in-law who smokes, yells at my grandson, shoves a greasy corn dog at him for lunch.

Hans did not offer to pay for the fish and chips, but fortunately Gardenia's thirty dollars covered lunch. Milo entertained them all with his new words—"refrigerator," "music"—and happily ate French fries and even some bites of coleslaw.

And Caitlin took Hans's hand as they walked back to the car.

Chapter Nineteen

THE DAY OF the department meeting Arnold fixed a substantial breakfast, two soft-boiled eggs and two pieces of whole-wheat toast and a large bowl of yogurt with some frozen blueberries. He did not want to be chewing on a sandwich during the noontime meeting, as some did, nor did he want to have a growling stomach.

Gardenia handed him a copy of the agenda when he arrived, but she did not stop to pet Leroy as she usually did and instead turned back to her computer. Arnold had noticed a change in her, a grimness or lack of luster that was striking because she usually was cheerful. As acting chair would it be his duty to inquire after her health or any other troubles she might have? No, it wasn't his business. She was, after all, a widow, with plenty of reasons to be glum. Best to say nothing and see if she returned to her usual gap-toothed-smiley self.

While he was making a cup of Keemun in the kitchenette, Frieda waved at him with her copy of the agenda.

"Arn, your name is under 'New Business.' Do you have some good news about your book?"

"Maybe soon. Dr. DuBarr will be putting in a good word for me with her editor at Yale." I will ask Laurel today about that, Arnold thought, before Frieda has a chance to mention it to her.

"That is so wonderful. I know you've been working on that book for a long time, and you deserve to have it published. I'm sure it's great."

"One would hope," he said as he swished the tea bag purposefully in the mug.

Laurel did not show up in the department offices that morning but rushed into the meeting just as it was about to start.

"Sorry, sorry. Page proofs and all that." She slammed her shoulder bag on the table. "I had my students do a take-home so I could have the morning off to finish up. My least favorite part of getting a book published, going over all the little things. I guess I'm just not a detail person."

Dodge said, "Since Dr. DuBarr has brought up the subject of publishing, I will cut to the chase, and so on. As I'm sure you are all aware, money is tight. The humanities are in competition with business and engineering for student enrollment."

"It's so unfair!" Frieda brayed.

Dodge was undeterred. "The question is, do we have enough money to support all the classes we offer in the English department? And it turns out, we don't. So to get right to the point, it has been decided that Professor Wiggens will no longer teach Chaucer but instead will join the ranks of freshman composition teachers. And as Wiggens has told me himself, composition is the essence of the English degree."

A soft gasp floated from the assembled department members.

"Oh, Arn!" cried Frieda, clasping her hands at her chest.

"Dr. Hamm, it is just business, as they say. No customers, your store closes. And Dr. Wiggens's shop has been teetering on bankruptcy, shall we say, for a few years."

Laurel said, "But his book is ready to be published."

"Is that right, Wiggens?"

"Under consideration," Arnold said softly. "Nothing definite."

Dodge continued, "Arn and I had a chat last week. He agreed with me that teaching composition will be an interesting challenge. He can use some of his Chaucer stuff to prompt essays, and so on."

Which was not at all what had transpired, Arnold thought furiously. You gave me a fait accompli, complete with debarned horses and debagged cats! You don't care if these students learn about one of the great authors of the English language, and you don't care about the years I've spent building up my curriculum and offering classes that no one else wants to teach.

But Arnold said nothing. What was there to say? The room was silent for a few moments, though Frieda sniffed as if holding back tears, before Dodge moved on to a discussion of requiring all graduating seniors to write a thesis. At the end of the meeting he mentioned the possibility of a new tenure-track opening in the department.

"That totally sucks," Laurel said as she walked beside Arn back to the English department offices. "And man, that bit about teaching composition? You can tell the Artful Dodger that you want your classes back."

Arnold smiled at her nickname for the dean. This was a woman with a sense of humor as well as other happy attributes.

"But at least it looks like I may be up for the tenure-track job. Why don't you come over to my place tonight?" Laurel said. "You can tell me more about your book."

"Sounds like a plan," Arnold said, pleased at the way this jaunty phrase came to the fore.

When Laurel opened the door to her second-floor apartment, an unfortunate gust from what might have been grilled hot dogs greeted Arnold.

"So this is my place. If I get a permanent job, I'll fix the place up. Have a seat."

Laurel gestured toward a maroon sofa that squatted in the middle of the room, facing a window that had a view of the neighboring building's roof. A large green metal trunk served as a coffee table. Laurel switched on a torchère. The dining room table was covered with what originally might have been a bedspread, an expanse of faded cotton with a pattern of marching elephants. Arnold sat on an Ikea chair that seemed standard issue for the homes of liberal arts colleagues.

"I haven't finished unpacking." Laurel pushed open the bedroom door. Against the wall were stacks of liquor-store boxes, on the bed a crumpled satiny blue duvet.

"Moving is one of life's least pleasant experiences," Arnold said.

"It sucks. But I have plans for this place. I've decided that my days of living like a grad school student are over—that's for sure. Another reason that I'm all about that tenure-track job."

"Which you richly deserve," he said, though she didn't seem to hear him as she busied herself depositing a large handful of potato chips on a small tarnished silver platter and pouring each of them a large glass of pinot grigio from a box.

Laurel sat on the sofa. The repetitious riffs of the Afropop music piping from her CD player made Arnold wonder, at first, if there was a scratch in the record. He remembered the days of LPs when this was a possibility. Laurel most likely did not.

She sat with her bare feet—larger and flatter than one would have imagined, with two conspicuous hammertoes—propped on the green trunk.

Sipping the pale wine, facing the pale beauty, Arnold searched for topics of discussion: the play at the Lakeshore Theatre, the weather, Laurel's UNW students. She in turn went on at some length about her latest book—which Arnold, being honest with himself, thought sounded tediously obtuse.

Finally she said, "Tell me about your book."

"The narrative rhythms of the tales. How they are structured. How they resemble each other. What Chaucer does to pique our interest."

"Yikes, that sounds pretty uh . . . uh . . . specific? I mean, an editor may not get who your target audience is."

"An academic study is its own reward." Arnold wasn't sure even as he heard the words what this meant. "May I ask, would you be willing to mention my manuscript to your editor?"

"Okay. He thinks my work is amazing, so maybe it will help."

"Thanks very much." Arnold knew that getting the proverbial foot in the door was not necessarily going to help if his book was just not good enough, which he thought might be the case.

"Now, how about some tips for getting tenure?" Laurel said.

"The application takes time. The most detailed CV you can come up with, and teaching evaluations. And a list of your many publications."

"No, no. All that's self-explanatory. What I want to know is, do I have to sleep with someone to get it?" At this she honk-laughed. "I mean, I hope to God it's not Dodge. OK, I was just kidding. But hey, if you end up on the committee, put in a good word, OK?"

"Ah, the committee," Arnold mumbled. How awkward, to be asked directly for a *good word!* Well, hadn't he done the same, requesting that Laurel mention his manuscript to her editor? But that was different—or was it?

He recalled the weeks and months before Frieda was granted tenure, when she had chatted up the committee members no matter where she had found them—copy machine or stairwell or Java Moose. Her sucking-up efforts had been so obvious, it was embarrassing, but she'd passed through the tenure checklist without difficulty: good student recs, class enrollment generally a half dozen or more bodies beyond the minimum, diligent presentation of papers at various conferences. Frieda had even published a selection of essays on Dylan Thomas that she'd collected and edited.

"I'm glad I met you right off, Arn." Laurel sat forward and leaned in his direction. "I mean, you are obviously such a smart guy, and you've been around long enough that you can share the inside dirt with me. So I was lucky."

"Why, thank you." Arnold saw from a small round plastic clock above the refrigerator that it was nearly ten. "It's late. I'll be on my way."

Laurel fairly leaped from the sofa.

"Oh, thank you for that. You know, I wasn't sure how things were going to go. I wanted to just hang out with you, and now I'm feeling completely wiped but didn't want to say the words *go to bed* and be misunderstood."

"You needn't have worried." Arnold carried his wineglass to the kitchen sink. "Thank you for your hospitality." He gave a shallow bow.

"Oh, Arn, you are such a throwback. Like you're rehearsing for a play or something. You know, *The Importance of Being Earnest* or whatever."

With that she curtseyed extravagantly and blew him a kiss.

Driving home, this blown kiss filled Arnold with wonder and confusion. Maybe it was a preamble for what their next date would involve. Or simply a dramatic gesture, as if she were taking the opposing part in a scene from the Oscar Wilde play.

I shall assume that a kiss of any sort is progress, he decided, whether or not such progress is appropriate between colleagues.

Chapter Twenty

Gardenia made it to the department store in the mall an hour before closing time.

She had some shopping to do before her date with Lex.

He had called her around two on Saturday. "Hey there. We talked about going dancing, so how about the swing dance at the Cascade Ballroom tomorrow night?"

Her response was several seconds of silence as she managed her surprise.

"Hello? Gardenia?"

If only he had availed himself of texting or even email, she could have composed herself before answering.

"Gardenia? Are you there?"

"Sorry, I had to think this through. What time?"

"Starts at eight thirty, or earlier if you want to take a lesson. You said you like to dance."

"I do, I do. All right, thank you. I'll meet you there at eight thirty. I'll get there on my own. In case I'm rushed for time."

Which she wouldn't be, but it was only prudent to drive herself.

She barely knew this man, their interactions limited to a chance meeting at a coffee shop, straining to hop under a limbo pole, and an evening at Frieda Hamm's. They had spent little time at the department party actually chatting with each other and ended the evening with an awkward handshake before they each returned to their respective cars. She hadn't seen him since then, as he had emailed her to say he would be out of town until mid-May.

She would pay for her own cover charge at the Ballroom, so she would owe him nothing.

Lex Ohashi is just another male acquaintance, Gardenia told herself, similar to the eccentric yet sweet Arnold Wiggens or odd, grief-addled Bruce or even Sylvie's exemplary husband, Doug.

Nonetheless, there she was, an hour later, in the women's lingerie department, which was tucked in a corner of the lower level of the store, so others would be less likely to see one furtively examining the padded bras or thongs.

It's just that I will *feel* more attractive if I'm wearing something lacy and not my usual one-hundred-percent-cotton underpants and my old beige sports bra, she thought. And besides, I need some new underwear.

"Are we finding what we need?"

A stout clerk dressed in a black skirt and lavender blouse, with thick red lipstick and large tan-framed glasses, chirped the question.

"I'm just looking."

"Something I could show you?"

"Well, maybe. I can manage by myself."

At this the clerk pointed to the round button on her jacket lapel, which read: *Arlene Beardsley, Certified Fittings Consultant.*

"Is it a bra you are looking for, dear? You're not alone in being shy about that. I'm trained to help customers find just the right fit. You'd be amazed, how many of us go most of our lives without finding the right size for the girls."

Arlene Beardsley glanced at Gardenia's chest. "It is so much easier to find a good fit when you're petite," she offered diplomatically. "I always hear some D-cup say how she wishes she didn't have so much in front."

"I wouldn't know about D cups. Except when I was nursing, I've always been an A."

"Believe me, you are one of the lucky ones." For emphasis, Arlene Beardsley straightened up and thus thrust her "girls" forward. A qualification for being a certified fittings consultant may have been to have a generous ramp of bosom yourself, no matter how others complained about their large breasts.

"We have a special this month, buy two and you get one free," Arlene went on, speaking over her shoulder as she led Gardenia to the racks of bras. "Some of my customers, they wait for this special to stock up. A red one, a white one, a black one." She winked and whipped a lacy black number off the rack. "Hmm—I'd guess you are an A, but the tape measure never lies."

Inside the fitting room, Gardenia took off her plaid cotton shirt, exposing her aging sports bra, and let Arlene Beardsley encircle her chest with a crisp yellow measuring tape.

"Well! You're a nice B, for sure. See, we don't get measured and go all these years with the wrong size."

"Sorry," Gardenia heard herself say as Arlene Beardsley waddled out of the dressing room and returned clasping a bouquet of lacy black bras on small plastic hangers.

"Thanks, I'll let you know which ones fit," Gardenia said.

"Usually customers let me fit them."

"Thank you, but I'll be fine." She did not want Arlene Beardsley's chubby fingers poking her.

Trying on the first one, Gardenia was startled at how sexy the black lace looked, the bra cut so that whatever cleavage one had was pushed up and shown off to advantage. Had Torre felt cheated by her low standards in the lingerie arena? Oh, she should have been more thoughtful about choosing sexy underwear! Soon after they were married, she had settled into serviceable cotton for underwear and pajamas.

Once Sylvie had given her a slinky nightgown in a deep wine hue for her birthday, adding some saucy note on the card about how this gift was for Torre. Gardenia had worn it to bed only once. The polyester fabric was itchy and hot. The following year, going through her closet and drawers to put together a bag for charity, she found the nightie and added it to the pile of old jeans and T-shirts. She knew that Sylvie never set foot in a thrift store so would never notice if her gift ended up on the Goodwill lingerie rack.

At the register Arlene said, "Well, at least you know you are a B, not an A." She rang up the sale on Gardenia's Visa and wrapped two black bras and one white one in tissue paper along with the matching underpants. "You deserve to know your cup size, I always say."

Perhaps Arlene reported to her husband each evening her cup-size successes, like a Jehovah's Witness bragging about a new convert.

"And hubby will be pleased, I can tell you that," Arlene said.

"Oh, mine's dead," Gardenia blurted.

"I beg your pardon, dear. I am so sorry! Me and my big mouth. It's just that the black lace is nearly always for someone else, if you know what I mean."

Driving home Gardenia was shocked to realize that she had just charged eighty-some dollars for these mélanges of lace and nylon. At least she had taken advantage of the buy-two-get-one-free discount, but what was she thinking? She had no business buying anything on credit.

How silly to spend so much on clothing items no one would ever see.

Torre had been a man of many virtues. Among these was not agility on the dance floor.

Three times Gardenia had coaxed him to take dance lessons, two for beginning swing and one for western line dancing. He had paced through the steps, while the instructors piped the counts on their head mics, with his face set in an expression most human beings use when on the way to the dentist.

Because she loved to dance, Gardenia had worked hard to follow his clumsy leading and had purred compliments at reasonable facsimiles of a correct move.

Finally he had put his foot down, so to speak.

"I'm sorry, Denie. But it's just not me. I can't feel the rhythm. I don't know why. I wish I could. I look around and there are all these other guys who get it. With their happy partners. Wish I could be one of them, but I'm not."

Gardenia had done her best to convince him that it was a matter of practice, but to no avail.

"I don't mind if you want to go by yourself. There are always some guys hanging around looking for partners," Torre had said. Once Gardenia had tried this, showing up for a swing dance at the Swedish Club, a reasonable choice because most of the dancers were midlife or older.

But when a portly bald guy had nearly yanked her onto the floor and huskily commanded her to "blend with my body," she had decided never again. She would dance with Torre or no one.

"That's why I'm going to the Cascade Ballroom with Lex," Gardenia told herself. "I like to dance. Nothing beyond that."

She decided to wear what Torre had called her Woodstock girl outfit: a gauzy gypsy skirt, a white peasant-style blouse with embroidery, and a crocheted shawl. At the last minute she pulled a box with a pair of cowboy boots from the bottom of her closet. She had bought these a few months after Torre had died, seeing them in a shoe shop window and rashly writing a check for $150.

They were bright turquoise blue, with medium-height heels and the classic pointed toes designed to jam into stirrups. Once home she'd put them on and walked around for about an hour, until her feet were screaming for release. She'd put them aside, thinking she'd return them, but never got around to it.

Tonight might be a good chance to break them in, Gardenia thought—not too many hours on my feet, and the smooth soles will slide on the dance floor.

Nervous about finding a parking place near the Ballroom, which was at the epicenter of Capitol Hill, she left early to give herself plenty of time to drive around and look for a spot. Anything to avoid those expensive parking lots, she thought, and I don't want to walk by myself in the dark at the end of the evening. Lex would offer to escort her, but still, best to keep her options open for independent coming and going.

Luckily she was able to find an empty spot across the street from the Ballroom, near the former Kentucky Fried Chicken shop, which oddly had survived for several years before closing, gasping its hot-fat breath into the hipsterism of the neighborhood.

Lex was waiting for her in the hallway outside the entrance to the ballroom. He wore suspenders with his striped pants, an appropriate costume for dancing to music from the swing era.

"Any trouble parking?" he asked, offering his hand.

"I found a free place by the old KFC," Gardenia said.

"Lucky you. I paid for a lot. Didn't think I'd have a choice."

The music was recorded, the dance floor only about two-thirds full. Oh, the feel of a man's hand on her back! And to move to the music, recorded though it was, and to spin and turn! Lex, it turned out, was a competent swing dancer who concentrated on his slim black oxfords half of the time rather than trying to make small talk. That's OK by me, Gardenia thought. The music is too loud for chit-chat anyway.

The other dancers included two slender young men in tight-fitting plaid shirts, dancing shyly together, as if for the first time, and some lesbian couples, and a tall transgender individual in a sequined dress.

"I am so glad to live in a time and place where all these different people can be couples and dance and no one even cares," Gardenia said to Lex during the break, testing him. He wiped the sweat from his brow with a white handkerchief.

"Something for everybody," he said.

By the second half of the evening the turquoise cowboy boots made themselves known. Her toes were nearly numb from the narrow toe box. She tottered and almost fell.

"Whoa. Something the matter?" Lex caught her. "Is it your boots? I wondered about those when I saw them."

Gardenia felt ashamed of her foolishness in thinking that the boots would make it through the evening.

"Maybe I'll sit down for a while," she said.

"OK. All right if I ask one of the wallflowers?"

"Sure."

Her chair at the edge of the dance floor was beside a window that faced the former KFC building. The Subaru waited under a streetlight. Dusk had settled in but on this soft spring evening the sidewalks were full of young people, escaping from their tiny apartments or shared houses, out to see and be seen.

A couple emerged from a shadow by the KFC. The young woman wore a bright red trench coat. Even in the semidark her thick blonde hair was obvious.

The man she was with—or should he be called a boy?—wrapped her in his arms and kissed her.

"Oh my God!" If not for the music, everyone in the room would have heard her. "Caitlin!"

Gardenia stood up and grabbed her shawl. I'll run out and confront her right now! she thought. She can't deny the truth!

But caution told her to look again. Now the two were strolling away toward the bookstore. The girl turned to look back at something just as they were passing under a streetlight.

Yes, it *was* Caitlin.

"Ready to try the next one?" Lex offered her a plastic cup of beer. "Not the best brew in town, but it's wet." He patted the back of his neck with the handkerchief.

"You know, I messed up by wearing these boots. My feet are killing me. I don't want to ruin your evening, but I'm going to excuse myself."

"Ah, too bad. Want to take them off?" Lex asked.

"No, that's all right."

"Mind if I stay? Seems the dancing goes on for another half hour or so."

"Yes, do carry on. You're a good dancer!"

She started to shake his hand but gave him a quick hug instead, her head turned to the side on his chest so there was no chance of a kiss.

Well-mannered man that he was, Lex insisted on escorting her down the long wooden staircase and out to the Subaru. She got into the car quickly to avoid any additional good-night gestures.

"We'll do it again," he said.

"OK. And I'll wear decent shoes."

I should have taken a picture of Caitlin with my phone, Gardenia thought as she drove home, her anger translating into a heavy foot on the accelerator. But no, that would be spying. Well, so what? Don't people hire detectives all the time to take photos of philanderers?

"See, sometimes it *is* zebras, not horses!" she nearly shouted, hoping that Torre, wherever he was, would hear.

Chapter Twenty-One

Just as Arnold was packing up on Friday afternoon and about to lock up his office and call it a week, Dodge sauntered up and leaned against the doorjamb.

"Wiggens, old man. I need to ask a favor," he said. "The tenure-track job. I thought maybe our new po-mo lady would qualify. But sadly, there's no money for a full-time tenure."

At the word *sadly* the dean hung his head.

"How about you break the news, old man?" Dodge slapped Arnold's shoulder. "As acting chair and mentor and so on. Closer to the ground, one could say. Part of the same flock. Rather than some high-and-mighty barging in." For the first time ever, Dodge knelt down and patted Leroy.

"Wait," Arnold said. "You held out the possibility, so you should be the one to tell her."

Dodge stood up and put his arm around Arnold's shoulders. "Help me out here, Wiggens. I'm thinking there will be some emotion. Not good with that. Crying and wringing the hands and so on. You two are friends. You'll know how to tell her. But soonish, if you know what

I mean. Thanks. Good man," Dodge continued, and left before giving Arnold a chance to reply.

He is your boss, Arnold reminded himself, and bosses get to tell you what to do, so you have no choice.

Arnold could not imagine Laurel crumpling into what Dodge saw as a typical female response to such news. She would snarl some four-letter words. But not directed at him—she would understand that Arnold was the messenger and would not blame him for this unfortunate development.

When, and how, to tell Laurel that she was yet again a one-quarter instructor, needing to look for work when the university year ended, her plans for fixing up her apartment for naught?

The appropriate time, occasion, and place will present themselves, Arnold reasoned.

Brunch at his mother's house that coming Sunday morning would not be the right time to tell Laurel the news.

Dorothy had invited Laurel, Frieda, and Arnold for nine thirty.

"That's pretty early for me, on a Sunday," Laurel had said. "I'm a night owl. I sleep in on the weekends."

"I could ask my mother about a later time," Arnold had offered.

"Naw, that's all right. I know older people get up early."

On Sunday morning, as he parked the Volvo down the block from the small View Ridge rambler where his mother lived, Arnold wondered if Laurel would appear at the appointed time. Dorothy Wiggens had considerable charm for her age, but she was nonetheless an eighty-one-year-old woman with nothing to offer Laurel DuBarr in terms of career advancement or even friendship. Laurel had agreed to the invitation before she had time to think, Arnold thought, and would call to beg off at the last minute.

The ardent Frieda, however, would arrive early.

"There you are. Laurel and I are having a fine time," Dorothy said when Arnold opened the front door. She sat next to Laurel on the couch, a large coffee-table book open across their laps.

Laurel had shown up right on time—how odd and yet exhilarating to see her sitting beside his mother.

"Your mother is a Cartier-Bresson fan just like me," Laurel said. "I've always wanted this book, but I forget that I want it until I see that someone else has it. Then I totally want it again!"

Dorothy laughed and patted Laurel on the shoulder. "Arnie, you didn't tell me that Laurel is a photographer. A shutterbug, as we used to say. Remember all those pictures I took on vacations? Daddy always complained about how much time I spent with my camera. I had to wait to get just the right shot."

"I used to have an old SLR film camera. I was a fiend in the darkroom," Laurel said.

"Ah, the creative flow," Arnold said. He imagined her amid the acrid fumes of developer solution and the clotheslines of damp prints, her hair pulled up in a mussed ponytail, apple cores and take-out cartons stacked on a countertop, a sleeping bag on a cot in the corner.

"I suppose we should go ahead and eat, before the food gets cold," Dorothy said. "Frieda called and said she was going to be late. Something about a meeting with students."

While Dorothy excused herself to the kitchen, Arnold whispered to Laurel, "Thanks for coming. My mother is a lovely woman, but many would not find a Sunday brunch with an octogenarian a thrilling choice."

"I always like meeting women who are older than I am but have still got something going on. That's who I'm going to be, for sure."

Laurel's slim elegance made Arnold notice anew his mother's living room: the aged sofa, the lumpy easy chair covered with a nappy throw, the framed art done by family friends and by the grade-school Arnold, the bookcase crammed with books, the dusty collection of small porcelain vases on the mantelpiece. The cotton rag rug was torn in a few places and even soiled. The woodwork needed a fresh coat of paint. Half-burned logs rested in the fireplace grate.

But Laurel's apartment is not a model of fine interior design, Arnold reminded himself. Maybe that's something she and my mother have in common.

Dorothy maneuvered the cast-iron skillet with its steaming frittata to the table and fetched a plate of carrot muffins.

"Cool dishes," Laurel said, holding up a heavy brown pottery plate. "I saw some of these in a vintage store."

"I bought a whole set, back in the seventies. With my first paycheck for my job as a library assistant at the grade school," Dorothy said. "You can't imagine how good that felt, a check with my name on it. Jerome told me to go out and buy whatever I wanted with that money."

"You mean you had to get his permission to buy these dishes?" Laurel plopped the plate back on the table.

"You see, I'd never had any money of my own. I had to ask Jerome if I wanted to buy something for myself."

"My father was a frugal fellow," Arnold said.

"I can't believe what women used to put up with," Laurel said. "Think of all the work women did at home, free labor all day long, and their husbands would leave them for someone younger and less overworked."

"Oh my, is that what your daddy did to your mother?" Dorothy leaned toward Laurel sympathetically.

"Not exactly. It's complicated."

"Mother, tell Laurel about your job at the library," Arnold said to change the subject, though he was curious about Laurel's family.

"Oh, I loved that job. All the little children!" Dorothy shared stories while they ate.

When they had finished eating, Arnold cleared the table and opened the old dishwasher, which was nearly full. He hoped the pile-up was not a sign of Dorothy's mental weakening. Her custom had always been to unload the washer before guests arrived.

Laurel and Dorothy were on the sofa again, this time with a large volume featuring Dorothea Lange photos, when Frieda rang the doorbell.

"I am so sorry I'm late. But you'll see why in a minute. Dorothy, so glad to see you." Frieda hugged Arnold's mother extravagantly but merely waved at Laurel.

"Dear, won't you have something to eat? A carrot muffin? Or some coffee?"

"Thank you, but I'm too excited to be hungry. Arn, sit down and I'll show you something."

He chose one of the straight-backed chairs by the dining room table. Frieda pulled a large manila envelope from her briefcase.

"Open it." She scooched up the sleeves of her gray fleece pullover and sat down beside him.

"Hey, it's not your birthday, is it?" Laurel asked.

"No, not unless it's July twenty-third and I didn't notice!" Dorothy said.

Inside the envelope was a carefully calligraphed proclamation.

"Well? Read it to us," Dorothy said.

"*Arnold Wiggens is a fine professor, and it would be a great loss to the* university if he no longer taught his excellent class on Geoffrey Chaucer. We, the undersigned students, hereby demand that he be allowed to continue his current teaching schedule. Others can teach composition, but few can teach us about Geoffrey Chaucer,"* Arnold read.

"Well now, isn't that nice?" Dorothy patted her son's shoulder. "But I don't understand, dear. I thought you always teach Chaucer."

"They decided they couldn't afford his classes and are going to make him teach composition instead." Frieda spoke as if Arnold were not sitting six inches from her. "The petition was *my* idea, but the students took it over. One of the sophomores did the calligraphy." Frieda beamed at Arnold. "What do you think, Arn?"

"It is not a matter of what *I* think," he said. "The powers that be have made their decision."

Laurel said, "It won't do any good. Dodge seems like the kind who does whatever people tell him he has to do. At least that might work in my favor, since they're telling him to offer me a tenure-track position."

"What? You mean you didn't hear? They've cancelled that. No replacement for Gludger. And maybe not any more of your po-mo." Frieda sprayed a mist of saliva as she said this last bit. "Someone was supposed to tell you."

Silence.

Dorothy picked up the proclamation and studied it. "I think it is just the nicest thing for you and the students to give Arnie a vote of confidence."

"Time for me to leave." Laurel picked up her bag. "Thanks for the brunch, Dorothy."

"You are most welcome, but going so soon?"

"I've got a busy day."

"Do come again. And we'll look at more photos."

Trailing Laurel to her car, Arnold said, "What a shock. And you would have been the perfect candidate if the position had been offered. This is disappointing for all of us."

Arnold braced for a stream of invective.

Laurel hunched over the open driver's-side door.

"I knew it was too good to be true! All this time going from one crap campus to another, and starting all over each year, and never the same apartment and never the same boss. Now it starts all over again." She banged her fist on the top of the car. "I'm so sick and tired of it. Fuck! I'm so sick and tired of it!"

"I'm so very, very sorry." Arnold started to put his arm around her but pulled back.

"It's not your fault. You're the only one who's been nice to me at all."

Again he started to offer a comforting hug, but she slipped into the driver's seat and closed the door before he had a chance.

Frieda had left by the time Arnold returned to the house, perhaps skulking out the back door because she was afraid of the consequences for the bearer of bad news.

"That Laurel is a smart young lady," Dorothy said, jamming the Cartier-Bresson book into the crowded lower shelf of the bookcase. "She said all kinds of clever things about Henri's photos."

Arnold said, "She's working on a second book. And she has asked our secretary to type up three journal articles in the past month. She's brilliant."

At least Arnold thought this was true. He was indisputably knowledgeable about Chaucer and his world, and Frieda Harm could quote poets from all the ages, and even Robert Gludger had received various teaching and scholarly awards. Laurel hadn't been around long enough for anyone to know how she would fare over the long haul.

"That's what I call prolific," Dorothy said. "And how about you, dear? How is your book coming? I always hate to ask, as I know you are sensitive about it."

"Coming along." He took the last of the plates from the dining room and started to wash them by hand, the dishwasher being full.

"I'm sure you are doing a fine job with your teaching," Dorothy said, "and they'll let you teach Chaucer again. But now tell your old mother—is Laurel your girlfriend? Must be. She seems plenty smart, but isn't she young for you? And not your type, I'd say. I feel sorry for those blonde girls. That pale skin, they'll start to show wrinkles by the time they're forty."

"We are colleagues and have known each other only since March," Arnold answered.

"I've always liked Frieda."

I refuse to continue this line of investigation, Arnold thought, and said, "I'll turn on the dishwasher for you before I leave."

"Frieda seems more like the wife type," Dorothy went on dreamily, picking at the last bits of frittata. "Something about Laurel makes me think she would wear thin as a wife."

"Enough on that topic." The dishwasher, clanging like a forge, nearly drowned out his crisp words.

"Oh, I'm sorry, dear. I try so hard to keep my mouth shut. Your father and I had such a nice life together. I want that for you."

Arnold gave his mother a quick hug. "Thanks for the brunch. Leroy is waiting for me. I'd better be off."

Walking down the block to the Volvo, Arnold passed a young

father with a towheaded toddler riding on his shoulders, the young mother's hand slipped through her husband's arm.

If Laurel and I had a child, what would he or she look like? Arnold found himself wondering. He imagined a blonde little girl, maybe with his curls but with Laurel's pale coloring.

Unbidden, an image of a little girl with Frieda Hamm's frenzied frizzy hair came to mind.

Well, that is *not* happening, he thought.

Crossing the Montlake Bridge, halfway back to Capitol Hill, Arnold remembered that he'd left the calligraphed proclamation on his mother's dining room table.

Chapter Twenty-Two

This, Gardenia thought, is what is called a bad day.

That morning she'd spilled some water on a freshly printed thirty-page draft for Laurel. Gardenia started to reprint it but discovered that the printer needed new toner. It would take an hour or more before someone could deliver it from the university warehouse.

Gardenia delivered the completed paper two hours late, which Laurel made clear she did *not* appreciate.

Frieda had chosen to stand by Gardenia's desk and blather on, on three different occasions, about her upcoming trip to the Oregon coast when the quarter ended in June. Gardenia usually could count on Arnold for cheerful and even entertaining conversation, but he had been distracted and didn't stop at her desk to chat. He nearly tripped over Leroy's leash and sloshed his mug of tea on the tile entry to the department offices.

Seattle Public Utilities had sent her a late-payment notice. She'd missed the due date for her credit card payment. A small container of deli salad that she'd bought for her lunch a few days before had spoiled in the office fridge, so she had to spend some of her precious cash at the campus food court.

And then there was the image of Caitlin in her red trench coat, embraced by someone-who-was-not-Hans in the shadow of the former Capitol Hill KFC.

Hans had asked her several weeks before to babysit Milo at her house on the last Wednesday of May, so he and Caitlin could have an at-home date night.

"I've signed up for the day off. We'll get some sort of fancy takeout and a bottle of wine and stay in," he had said, rather proudly and maybe even defiantly, as if to prove to Gardenia that all was well with the two of them.

Gardenia had readily agreed and would keep her promise even though she wished she could back out—she wanted more time to compose herself before seeing Hans in person. *That's what Torre would tell me to do,* she thought. *He'd say to make sure I think through carefully what I'm going to say so I don't blurt out words that will make the situation worse.*

On the other hand, any time with precious Milo would be soothing.

Gardenia answered the sharp knock on her front door to find only Caitlin and Milo.

"Oh, Hans is in the car?"

"No, plans have changed. I've got to help with a study session, so I brought Milo by on my way. Hans is going to hang out at home. Probably on the couch playing video games."

A snort, that's how anyone would describe the sound that Caitlin made when she said this.

Gardenia's anger flared like a blowtorch, and she wanted to bark, *He works lots of extra hours, and he does extra duty with Milo, so I'd say it's OK if he wants to be a couch potato sometimes.* Fortunately Milo reached for his grandma, distracting Gardenia from saying this and other more furious words.

"Must be nice to have friends to study with," Gardenia managed. Were I a detective—and maybe I *am* a detective—I would be watching this faithless creature's eyes, to determine whether Caitlin is lying, she thought. I would be able to tell from some flicker of the eyelids, or the rictus of her smile, that she was fibbing.

"Yep. Group projects are the way it's done."

Caitlin kissed Milo good-bye and hurried out to the car. She pulled the red trench coat from the back seat of the Toyota and put it on before climbing into the driver's seat.

I saw you in that coat, kissing a man in front of the old KFC, Gardenia could have called out matter-of-factly to Caitlin, as if she were reporting some news she'd heard on the radio about a road construction project or a string of stormy days in the offing.

No, it would be disaster to confront Caitlin, Gardenia told herself—your son's marriage is none of your business. If you want to keep seeing Milo, you'd better keep your mouth shut.

Milo had just fallen asleep in the portacrib when Gardenia's cell pinged.

"Hey, Ma," read the text. "Caitlin sez staying nite w/Ashley. Will pick dude up @ 8."

"Staying the night with Ashley"—ha! Didn't the hussy even have enough imagination to think of another ruse?

Surely Hans had his suspicions, but oh denial, seductive denial, such a potent force in human life!

Hans showed up just before eight as planned, ever the well-trained musician who knew that "Early is on time, on time is late, and late is unacceptable."

"The sweetie pie just fell asleep. Do you have time for some tea?"

"Sure."

Gardenia poured each of them some decaf English breakfast. "Sorry the date night didn't work out."

"Oh well. At least she cares about getting good grades."

"Well, you know I am always happy to help out. If you want to leave Milo with me some evening next week."

"Thanks, Ma."

The silence sat between them like a big Maine coon cat.

Hans grabbed a banana from the hanging basket by the sink and crammed big chunks in his mouth. Jamming the banana peel into the compost waste bucket on the counter, he rumbled, "I've had it."

"Oh?" He knows, Gardenia thought, he knows she's cheating! And now he's going to tell me, and I will listen calmly and wisely . . .

But instead Hans said, "Those bins, no one seems to care!"

"*Bins?*"

"The bulk bins! The way they're designed, half of them spill out, and there's always a mess, split peas all over the floor. Which I always seem to clean up, because nobody else bothers. But does anyone ever notice and thank me? Nooooo. Lark doesn't have the time to clean up, but she has plenty of time to chat with the new checker, when he's on his way to the back room for his break." Hans pulled open the refrigerator door and found a piece of string cheese, which he ripped into skinny threads.

"*Lark?*"

"The new supervisor. Moved over from the other store. One of those old hippie types who's been working there forever and thinks she's younger than she is. Tattoos up the ying-yang and dreads." Hans looked at Gardenia. "Mom, I'm guessing she's about your age, by the look of her skin and all. Though maybe she was a California girl."

"Well, bosses are a challenge."

"I just wish I didn't have to work there, Mom! But I don't see what choice I have. I've got to keep a steady job while Caitlin's in school. And we need the health insurance."

"You could finish up your degree, teach or something?" Oh no, the slippery slope of unsolicited advice! But she couldn't stop herself, a bowling ball careening down the slick wooden alley.

"How can I go back to school? I'm not going into debt for tuition, that's for sure, and someone's got to look after the little man. Day care is expensive."

"I wish I didn't have to work full time. I could take over with Milo and you could go back to school. Maybe you could get a scholarship. You had one your freshman year, why wouldn't they give you one again?" The cascade of words was impossible to stop.

Hans glowered at her. "Mom, that's enough. You know I've barely practiced since Milo was born. No way I could walk in and get any money from anyone for some half-baked audition piece. It's just Green Thumb Natural Foods Co-op for me, for the rest of my life. Woo-hoo!"

Gardenia tried two slow nods of understanding.

Hans took her empty mug and his and rinsed them out under the full rush of the tap.

"Caitlin didn't come home last night either," he said.

"Oh?"

"Studying for midterms with Ashley. She does that a lot."

"Um, students have to study." Gardenia opened the dishwasher for Hans so he could load the mugs.

"Midterms happen once a quarter, right? She always calls them midterms, like she forgets that she already took them two weeks before. Anyway, I've got to get the kid home and in bed and get some sleep myself."

"Sure you don't want to leave him here overnight? You could stay here."

"Naw. I'd better get him home."

Now she was racing downhill on a bicycle without brakes.

Gardenia heard herself say, "Honey, I have something to tell you."

Hans straightened up, a flash of fear on his face.

"Mom, are you sick?"

"It's not about me. It's about Caitlin."

"She's sick? No she's not! She would have told me."

"It's not that she's sick. I don't know how to say this except to just say it. A week ago Sunday I went to the Cascade Ballroom on Capitol Hill with this guy."

"Rock on, Mama! Who is it? Somebody from the college?"

"No, I met him at Café Venezia, in Pioneer Square. Before that special spring art walk."

"Wait. Maybe I should meet him. Just to read the guy vibe. If you know what I mean." He folded a stick of gum in his mouth and chewed noisily. "Dad would want me to keep tabs on any men who are showing an interest. I mean, he would want you to see people, but he wouldn't want you to go out with some creep."

"No, no, nothing to worry about. I mean, who knows if I'll even go out with him again? Hey, Hansie, I have to tell you something that I don't want to tell you and I don't know how to tell you so I'll just tell you. When we were leaving, I saw Caitlin standing on the corner next to the old KFC across the street from the Cascade Ballroom."

"It couldn't have been Caitlin. She *hates* KFC." He added a second stick of gum to the one he was chomping on. "Wait, that one's closed down, isn't it? Maybe she was coming back from Ashley's. She lives on the Hill."

"She wasn't with Ashley. She was with a man."

"So? Maybe just another one of her classmates. Why do you care?"

"Honey, he wasn't acting like a classmate."

Milo, as if sensing the tension in the kitchen even from his porta-crib in the spare bedroom, began to whimper. Hans fetched his son and took him to the front door wrapped in the acrylic blanket with an airplane motif that he himself had used as a child.

"Mom, I need to set some boundaries. It's not OK for you to criticize my wife, ever. Or make up stories about her. And I mean it."

"Oh, honey, you know I'm not the type to make up a story about someone. I saw her, in her red trench coat."

"Lots of women have red trench coats. You've never liked her, but this is just too much."

"I'm sorry I said anything! I was way out of line. Let's pretend this never happened. I must be dealing with more than I think I am. Messes up my judgment. Forgive, OK?"

"Mom, I'm taking Milo home." Hans let Gardenia hug them but pulled the door closed as he left in what could have been considered a slam.

Of course Hans would take Caitlin's side! Now both Hans and Milo would be ripped out of her life, never to return. Her need to tell the truth had torpedoed her connection to her only son and only grandson.

Torpedo—yes, the word was so apt, with its image of sudden and irreparable destruction.

The next morning Hans did not pick up when she phoned him, nor did he answer her sprightly text: "Hi Hon! I do apologize again for what I said and will be more careful in the future! Can I drop by tomorrow? XXOO"

Well, he was busy with Milo and would respond later, she figured. Or maybe his phone was out of juice—it's easy for a busy young father to forget to charge his phone.

All day long she checked for texts and emails but found nothing from Hans. Lex texted, suggesting another dance date. "My weekends are pretty full, will be in touch," she texted back.

When she got home that evening after work, Gardenia changed into her gray sweatpants and an old T-shirt from one of Hans's high school band trips. These clothes are a fitting metaphor for what's going on in my life, she thought, though I'm not sure exactly how.

Susie gyrated with joy when Gardenia said, "Shall we go for a walk?" I should be more like my dachshund, she thought as she watched Susie happily sniffing the weeds and grass at the edge of the sidewalk. Whatever is in front of her, there she is, enjoying it.

A determined breeze tossed the grand lilac bush in a neighbor's yard. Just smell the lilacs, she told herself. Stay in the moment and let go of all that worry—let go of things you can't control.

A car trundled down the street and pulled over. A face peered out from the window on the driver's side.

Gardenia started to walk more quickly, pulling Susie behind her, until she saw it was Sylvie's friend Bruce, wearing a cat burglar's black watch cap.

"I found you! Sylvie gave me your address, and I was in the neighborhood, so I tried calling but you didn't pick up. I knocked on your door. I was going to ask you out for a quick bite."

"I saw the call but didn't recognize your number, so I didn't answer it. I'm walking Susie now."

"I'll wait for you to take the doggy home." Bruce's confidence made her feel both annoyed and pleased, though she didn't understand the latter. Well, when they'd first met at Sylvie's barbecue, he'd given her an open invitation to talk about Torre. I don't mind taking him up on that, Gardenia thought.

"Well, OK. I'll take Susie home."

"Sounds good. I'll park in front of your place."

OK, she would have dinner with Bruce, but she wouldn't change out of her sweatpants, and she'd watch her body language carefully so as not to give him the wrong idea. She'd pay for her own meal and would make sure that they took equal turns talking about Torre and Janine.

Bruce chose a small Indian restaurant in the Roosevelt neighborhood a short drive from Gardenia's house. A young waitress in a sari led them to a far booth by a window and handed them menus.

"Janine liked to cook but she got tired of it, so she liked to eat out. But I was never wild about it. Expensive, and when the kids were little, it seems we spent the whole meal trying to keep them from making a mess or having a meltdown."

"We took Hans to a Chinese place once when he was about two. He did pretty well, so we thought we were such great parents," Gardenia said.

"You can't believe that your kids will ever be teenagers when they're little," Bruce said.

"Or that one day they'll be twenty-four, married, and with a child," Gardenia added, and glancing up from her menu, she saw that Bruce was looking at her. "Something wrong?" she asked.

"No, no. It's just that I haven't sat across the table from an attractive lady in so long."

Gardenia was grateful that the waitress walked up at that moment with the two pale ales they had ordered. The girl was about Hans's age, she guessed, with the luminous dark eyes that seemed standard-issue in India, and a slender wedding band. An older, stouter woman, also in a sari and with an armful of gold bangles, appeared from the back of the restaurant, holding a chubby baby boy a bit younger than Milo.

"Excuse me, but I guess I'm needed," the waitress said as she took the child and handed the older woman the order pad.

"Pardon my daughter-in-law," the woman said. "Her boy's hungry. There are some things we grannies can't help with, you know."

"Your first grandchild?" Gardenia's motive in posing this question was to bring up the subject of her own beautiful Milo, perhaps even share the photos on her iPhone.

"My first son's first son."

"My son has a son, about the same age."

"So you know how nice it is. Seeing your son as a father." The woman smiled, and Gardenia guessed from her soft, plump face that she was only in her forties, ten or more years younger than Gardenia herself.

"Though we still worry, don't we? Even about a grown-up son," Gardenia offered.

"We never stop being mothers." The Indian grandmother sighed and shrugged. "What can I get you?

"Butter chicken, please," Bruce said. "And the Kashmiri rice. Oh, and some samosas to share."

"And you, ma'am?" Now the woman had composed herself as a waitress and restaurant owner, no longer a confidante. Gardenia ordered a vegetarian dish with tomatoes and chickpeas.

Bruce pulled out a thick worn wallet and extracted a photo of a woman in an orange sweater, posing by an arrangement of what looked like yellow mums. "That's Janine. She bought that vase at the University District Street Fair. Two hundred dollars, I think it was. Let's just say I wasn't pleased. But a few years later, the woman who made it got some sort of artist's award and her prices went way up. So I ate crow."

Gardenia said, "The orange sweater and yellow flowers—she liked color?"

"Red, orange, yellow. Stayed away from the blues and browns. Said there were enough dull colors in the Northwest. She could have been an artist herself, the way she decorated the house."

As Gardenia bit into one of the hot samosas, part of the filling tumbling out onto her plate, she wondered if this was the start of an exchange of dead spouse stories.

Bruce carefully cut the last of the three samosas in half.

"I cut, you choose," he said.

Gardenia took the smaller piece, surprised that he found this childish ritual necessary. Torre would have offered her the entire samosa or automatically taken the smaller piece for himself.

Bruce said, "Eating alone is a drag. So thanks for coming out with me tonight."

"You're welcome."

"Not a bad butter chicken," Bruce said. "Try some." He pushed the small tureen toward her. The three stars of spiciness did not mask what seemed to be condensed Campbell's tomato soup mixed with cream.

Bruce chewed and swallowed, took a swig of beer, put his fork down, and lowered his head into his hands.

"Are you OK?"

"She did a big Indian meal once, for my birthday," Bruce mumbled, using a thumb to brush away tears. "And I was such a low-down fool that I told her later that the butter chicken wasn't that good."

The clatter of plates from the kitchen and the wail of a toddler wiggling to get out of his high chair masked Bruce's muffled sobs. Gardenia was facing the rest of the room, the weeping Bruce not visible to the other diners.

She handed him a tissue from a crumpled package in her purse.

"Man, didn't think it was going to hit me tonight. Why the hell did I order butter chicken?" He shoved his plate aside and wiped his eyes. "I keep remembering all the stupid things I said. The mean things. And now I can't say I'm sorry."

"She knew that you loved her," Gardenia suggested, though she was beginning to think that Bruce was on the selfish side, compared with a man like Torre. You learn a lot from the way a person deals with the last samosa, she thought. If anything, she had been the impatient one in her marriage, but she had always been quick to apologize.

Gardenia raised her hand for the bill while Bruce excused himself and headed for the exit. When she joined him outside, he looked so miserable, his eyes red and his cap askew on his head, that she hesitated to mention to him what his share cost.

"This should cover it," he said, fortunately, before she had to ask, handing her a twenty and a five.

Bruce turned the volume up on the local jazz radio station during the ride home. Gardenia was grateful that the blare of "All of Me" filled the car and made small talk unnecessary. Pulling up in front of Gardenia's house, Bruce said, "Crying in a restaurant, didn't expect that."

"I completely understand. Thanks for the invite." As Gardenia started to open her door, Bruce lunged and grabbed her arm.

"Gardenia, aren't you as lonely as I am?" His eyes were bright, his breath smelling of garlic.

"That's *enough*." She wriggled loose and jumped out of the car, and, maddeningly well-bred person that she was, found herself turning back to the car to wave.

He rolled down the window and called out, "Sorry, didn't mean to be out of line."

"But you were!" she shouted from her doorstep. "You *were*!"

Why did I think that this invitation was so innocent, just a couple of middle-aged acquaintances eating butter chicken and samosas and feeling sorry for themselves? she scolded herself. I am so out of touch.

I don't know how to deal with men.

I don't know what I should be doing with my life, or when I'll stop missing Torre.

I don't know when my son will speak to me again or when I'll see my precious grandson.

Susie whimpered joyously when the front door opened.

At least I have you, Gardenia thought, my sweet little dachshund. And you love me, no matter what.

Chapter Twenty-Three

GARDENIA WOKE AT six thirty even though it was Saturday and she had not set her alarm. She pulled on her plaid flannel robe and opened the back door for Susie, and while heating the teapot she recalled, now fully awake, the reason for the sad ache in her heart.

It was the first Saturday in June, and she not heard from Hans for a week and a half.

She had sent him several cheerful texts, but no replies zinged back to her.

Maybe he needed a short break from contact with his mother, she reasoned, to "process his feelings," as a therapist would say.

She would be patient and try to control her obsessive checking of texts and emails. At least she could leave the actual mailbox alone, as no one sent important news by snail mail anymore.

In her stained gardening jeans and shirt she spent an hour turning over the soil in the two parking-strip beds she used for vegetables. The tulips that she massed in a third parking-strip bed had long ago dropped their petals, only the skinny bare stems now poking up, the shriveled leaves having done their work of feeding the bulbs so there would be new blooms next spring. A metaphor there somewhere, Gardenia thought, which someone in the English department would be happy to unearth for me.

She cut a last sprig of lilac and found a vase for it in the cabinet above the fridge. Hans had made this chubby little ceramic pot as part of a middle-school summer camp—had she been appreciative enough of his effort? He had brought it home so proudly. She couldn't recall the last time she'd displayed it on the kitchen table. From now on she would keep the vase on the table, filled with seasonal blooms, so that Hans could see it when he came over.

If he ever came over again.

Gardenia had not told Sylvie about her foolish decision to bleat to Hans what she had seen at the KFC. She felt ashamed that her son was in such a messy situation—was it somehow her fault? But after lunch Gardenia changed out of her gardening clothes and impulsively drove to Sylvie's place. I have to talk with someone, she thought. Sylvie will listen.

Her friend did not answer the doorbell on the first ring, nor the second, nor the third. Maybe she and Doug were out. But no, the Mini Cooper was in the driveway. Just as Gardenia was about to leave, Sylvie opened the door.

"Oh, Denie. I guess I forgot that you were coming over?" Sylvie's thick dark hair was flecked with what looked like bits of Styrofoam. She wore an old canvas shirt that Gardenia had seen Doug put on to do yard work.

"You didn't forget. I just wanted to stop by and say hi. But you look like you're in the middle of something."

"Kind of. Sorting through stuff in kitchen cabinets and upstairs closets."

"I should get busy and declutter my place. Want some help?"

"Well, sure. But it's tedious, I'm telling you."

But tedium was not what Gardenia felt after fifteen minutes of wrapping china dessert plates and coffee cups and saucers in newspaper and handing them to Sylvie to pack in a cardboard box from the liquor store. Instead she felt a cold sensation in her belly, dread or fear or confusion or some of all three.

"Why are you storing these?" she asked. "You don't use them?"

"Not so much anymore," Sylvie said, not looking at Gardenia. "I think I'll take them to Goodwill."

"Those stacks of books in the living room too?"

"Doug is on a clean-out rampage too. He's taking those to a used bookstore." Sylvie reached into a large plastic garbage bag full of Styrofoam peanuts and packed them around the china before turning to Gardenia. "Sorry, I didn't ask why you dropped by. Something you want to talk about?"

Why being asked directly to share something always made Gardenia want to clam up, she wasn't sure, but her first impulse was to say "Oh, nothing, just wanted to hang out." Sylvie kept looking at her, though.

"Caitlin is for sure cheating on Hans."

"Denie, what? How do you know that?"

"I saw her. With some guy. Outside the old KFC on Capitol Hill. She had on that red trench coat, the one without a hood. Crazy choice in this climate."

"Does Hans know?"

"Yes, because I told him. Now he hates me and doesn't answer my texts. And I'll never see Milo again!"

Sylvie hugged Gardenia awkwardly as they sat on the floor in front of the dining room hutch, but she got up to answer a sharp rap on the front door.

"Denie, this is awful, and I want to hear more about it all, but that's the movers."

"*Movers*? I know you guys have talked about downsizing, but you didn't tell me you'd found a new place. One of those condos near Green Lake that you like?"

"Let me get them started on the stuff in the garage."

While Sylvie directed the movers, Gardenia gently wrapped some crystal goblets that she and Torre and Hans had used many times at Sylvie's Thanksgiving gatherings. The real estate market was heating up, with not much inventory, so Sylvie and Doug must have grabbed something that came up for sale and hadn't had a chance to tell anyone about it.

When Sylvie returned Gardenia said brightly, "A change for you but hey! Less house to worry about and a new neighborhood to explore. If it's one of those Green Lake places, it'll be easy to walk the lake and catch up."

"Not a condo, Denie. Not by Green Lake." Sylvie avoided Gardenia's gaze. "Not here. Doug got a job in Santa Fe."

"What?" Gardenia wailed. "That's why Doug went back and forth to Santa Fe! Why didn't you tell me?"

"Believe me, I said no when Doug first got the offer. You were one of the reasons I don't want to move. I told Doug I wasn't sure what you'd do without me—I mean, what you and I would do without each other. I guess I thought I'd wait a while to tell you, since you'd just started that new job and had a lot on your mind."

"How is Esme going to cope? She's used to depending on you two. Even though she's all grown up and going to medical school." Gardenia heard the barb in these words but couldn't stop herself from saying them.

"One of those coincidence things. She got a University of New Mexico residency, starting in the fall. Albuquerque. So she'll be close by." Sylvie put her hands on Gardenia's shoulders and looked at her. "I'm so sorry about Hans and Caitlin. He'll come around. You're such a good mom. And a marvelous grandmother. I envy you that little Milo, what a darling child."

Thanks, Sylvie! Gardenia wanted to yell. *Thanks a lot! You are always so, so kind, even when you're telling me, your dear friend, that you're abandoning me.*

But Gardenia managed to ask a half dozen questions about Santa Fe and Doug's job and their new house before excusing herself for home.

There was no Torre.

There was no Hans.

There was no Milo.

Soon there would be no Sylvie.

She was alone, alone, alone.

But moaning and crying isn't going to help, Gardenia told herself. You've got to deal with all of this and keep going.

She would use the *Industry is the enemy of melancholy* cure once again. Warmed up by helping Sylvie pack, she sorted through her own dining room hutch. An hour later she had a box of teacups, an embroidered tablecloth inherited from her mother, a delicate Japanese vase that had been a gift from one of Torre's visiting colleagues, and a pewter cream-and-sugar set.

I'll take these to that vintage store in Fremont, see if I can sell them for something, she thought—I could use some extra cash and it feels good to get rid of stuff.

In the basement she found a tan hard-sided plastic suitcase that her parents had given her before she went to college. How many times she had painfully lugged it through airports, before someone finally figured out that luggage should have wheels! I suppose this has sentimental value, as a launch gift from my parents, she thought, but I will never use it again.

The universe offered her a parking place right in front of the Fremont vintage consignment mall. She made two trips down the stairs, one with the box and the other with the suitcase.

Behind the antique cash register at the checkout counter was a framed vintage sign: *Street Girls Who Are Entertaining Sailors Must Pay in Advance.*

Caitlin's paramour, glimpsed in the gloaming by the KFC, did not appear to be a sailor, but wasn't that exactly what her daughter-in-law had been doing? *Entertaining* a man, whether at a hotel or his flat? The only difference being that it was all about *love*, and not a commercial transaction.

"I've got some things to sell," Gardenia said to the young woman at the counter, who had a lip ring and spiky dyed-black hair.

"Oh, sorry. Saturday's not a buying day," she said.

"Can I leave these things here until Monday?"

"Sorry, we don't have room to store stuff. And we're not open on Monday. Tuesdays work."

Gardenia picked up the tan suitcase to haul it back to her car. Near an arrangement of vintage kitchenware, a familiar voice said, "I had a hand-crank beater just like this, honey, don't you remember? And look at this KitchenMaid cupboard! That wasn't from my time. We had real built-in kitchen cabinets and thought we were so la-di-da. But my mother had one of these. Up-to-the-minute at the time. Look at all these little drawers. And the storage bin for flour."

"Indeed, a relic of the homemaking era."

Gardenia could have crept up the stairs to the sidewalk and her car and not said anything to Arnold Wiggens and his mother, as their backs were toward her. But she stopped and called out, "Fancy meeting you here!"

Arnold looked up from the box of old postcards he'd started to examine. "Ah! What a pleasant surprise! Mother, this is the administrative assistant who works for the department, Gardenia Pitkin." He gestured toward his mother. "And my mother, Dorothy Wiggens."

"We've spoken on the phone several times, haven't we?" Gardenia said as she shook Dorothy's small cool hand.

"Yes we have. And you have excellent phone manners, my dear," Dorothy said. "*Gardenia*. It's been a long time since I've met someone with a flower name. There used to be *Daisys* and *Irises* all over the town."

"I hear those names are having a comeback," Gardenia said.

"Before you know it there may even be a baby Dorothy."

"*Dorothy* is such a nice name," Gardenia said, though it was not her favorite, always bringing to mind Judy Garland in her gingham dress, skipping along the yellow brick road.

"Let me help you with that," Arnold said, taking the suitcase from Gardenia and whispering, "Mother always enjoys an outing to a vintage store."

Gardenia opened the back hatch of the Subaru, pushed aside some canvas grocery bags and a package of toilet paper that she had inexplicably forgotten to carry into the house, and let Arnold load the suitcase.

"We were able to land men on the moon before they figured out how to put wheels on suitcases," Gardenia heard herself say and qualified the observation. "Although that's not my original thought."

"So true, nonetheless. You plan to use this for some upcoming travels?"

"Oh no, I was hoping to sell it but apparently it's not a 'buying day.'" Somehow she didn't feel sheepish sharing this with Arnold. "I have another box of things down by the register."

"Shall I fetch it for you?"

"No, no, I can do it. You should get back to your mother. I salute you for bringing her here."

"She finds things that she remembers from her childhood and tells stories about them. I serve as her audience," Arnold said.

"I have to say, you must be the world's best son."

"Ah, now that is an overstatement, but thank you. Your son would do the same for you. You are planning to enjoy his company this weekend? And your grandson's?"

"Not exactly. See you on Monday!" Gardenia felt tears spring to her eyes, so she hurried down the stairs to retrieve her box. Arnold joined his mother, who was still examining antique kitchenware.

"I do think I could use some of those glass refrigerator containers," Dorothy was saying to her good, kind son as Gardenia hauled her box up the stairs to the Subaru. "I have to put my leftovers in something, so why not a little dish that reminds me of my dearly departed mother?"

Chapter Twenty-Four

FRIEDA PRESENTED THE petition to Dodge with a trio of students from Arnold's class, but there was no response from the dean. Meanwhile Arnold carried on as usual with his Chaucer teaching and offered only a few words of thanks to the students for their effort. He would not make a fuss about the petition, as the dean might think the students were helping Dr. Wiggens in exchange for good grades.

After the fateful brunch and the news that Laurel would not be offered a tenure-track position, the adjunct po-mo professor had made herself scarce. She slipped in and out of the office to check her mail but did not stop to chat and barely even waved at Arnold when she passed him on the campus pathways.

Laurel is avoiding others as she deals with her disappointment and invective-worthy anger, Arnold reasoned.

Oh, how he had felt for Laurel as she had leaned over the open car door, the self-assured, brilliant, and stunning young professor reduced to a human being like all the rest! *I will be there for you!* he declared to himself, though the words made him cringe, for he must have heard them on some piped-in pop song in an elevator or department store.

I'll send Laurel an email and suggest strolling over to the Java Moose for coffee, he thought. I'll listen to whatever she wants to tell me about this change in her situation, and from there who knows what might happen?

But on Friday, before leaving for the weekend, he boldly emailed her, and rather than suggesting coffee, wrote: "A light repast at my place on Sunday evening, perhaps?" To his surprise, she replied almost immediately: "Sure, what's your address?"

Arnold chose Sunday because he could avail himself of the weekly Broadway Farmers Market, which must have drawn more congregants than all the churches in the neighborhood combined. The freshest ingredients, simple yet elegant preparation, some gâteaux and baguettes from a French bakery—why, he would do all his shopping on foot, as if a Parisienne, and would regale Laurel with what he saw and overheard while on his errands.

As festive as the market was, however, the farmers still had little to offer in early June. Early greens, sugar snap peas, some small new potatoes, leeks that might have overwintered, apples that had waited out the cold season in a warehouse near Yakima. He would make potato leek soup à la Dorothy Wiggens and a salad with arugula and baby lettuce, and he'd grill a steak on his back deck.

Arnold decided to return home to unload the bag of produce before walking in the other direction to the bakery. Leroy would be happy to see him and could trot along beside him to the bakery. Passing through Cal Anderson Park, Arnold felt the guilt that often flickered within him as he noted the winos and young street people lounging in their greasy jackets, with matted hair and worn-out shoes. A police car stationed at the side entrance to the park acknowledged the hazards of mixing Capitol Hill hipsters and people of all races, gender identities, and sexual preferences with the homeless and the inebriated. A country as bursting with prosperity as the United States and still, so many had so little, or were pulled down into a vortex of unemployment and mental illness and substance abuse.

He would ask Laurel what she thought should be done, what two well-educated and privileged individuals such as themselves could do to ameliorate the troubles of others less fortunate. Yes, their relationship could expand to accommodate all sorts of topics of conversation as well as—it was possible—other earthier delights.

Distracted by thoughts of sitting with Laurel on his deck, each sipping a predinner gin and tonic and listening to some vintage Dave Brubeck wafting from the living room, he did not turn on his usual vigilance at the sight of two young men by the alley gate to his backyard.

"Let's give him a hand with those groceries."

"No need. Have a good day." Now Arnold felt the adrenaline rush. It was broad daylight, but there were two of them, and the green Dumpster blocked the gate from the view of anyone passing on the nearby sidewalk.

"Naw, I mean it. We'll give you a hand. This where you live?"

The guy had a missing front tooth and startlingly blue eyes. He stank of whatever cheap alcohol he had been drinking and the sourness of the need for a shower.

His companion, shorter and with a head of dark hair tied back in a ponytail, grabbed the canvas bag.

"Got any beer, my friend? Or weed?"

"We'll settle for cash." Blue Eyes grabbed Arnold's arm and hissed the words with his fetid breath. "Hand it over."

From his pocket Arnold pulled two twenties and a handful of change. Presciently he had not taken his debit card, only enough cash for what he planned to buy. This will be over in a moment, he told himself, but time slowed down as Blue Eyes counted the money.

Wasn't he supposed to scream, or fight back, or run? Or was compliance the best choice, the safest choice?

"Not all that much, eh, buddy? So why don't we take a little peek at your place and see what else you might have to share with us?"

"Bet he's got some mighty fine wine in there somewhere. He looks like the wine type, wouldn't you say?" The short one clapped Arnold on the back and pushed him toward the locked gate. "After you, my friend."

"No. I'm not letting you in. Take the money and get out of here."

"Whoa, whoa, getting a little ballsy here, aren't we?" Blue Eyes had not pulled out a knife or gun. Yet.

"If he don't want visitors, I'd say we'll let it go for now," Shorty said. "Middle of the day and all. Don't want to make a fuss." He upended the canvas bag, sending the potatoes rolling down the alley, the leeks and greens landing in a heap that he squashed with his grubby sneaker.

"We do want to give him something in return, though, don't we?" With that Blue Eyes smacked Arnold in the face, sending him tumbling against the rickety wooden fence. "And hey, we know where he lives, don't we?"

Arnold's face throbbed with the blow, which had landed just below his left eye. Was his cheekbone shattered?

"See ya later, if you know what we mean," Shorty said.

The two sauntered down the alley toward the sidewalk.

"Help," Arnold called weakly. "*Help!*" His face felt warm where the fist had made contact. With his index finger he checked for blood, but the skin wasn't broken. He ran his tongue over his front teeth—at least the blow hadn't hit his mouth. With shaking hands he opened the gate, locked it behind him, and bounded up the stairs to his apartment.

Arnold held the happily wriggling Leroy as he collapsed on the sofa. His hands trembled, his body felt jazzed from fear and shock. I'll call the police, he thought. But if they pick up the two and charge them, he would have to identify them and thus be vulnerable should they be let out on bail or acquitted. It was his word against theirs, and, as they had pointed out, "We know where he lives."

They could come back at any moment, for that matter, to hassle him. Or worse.

A knock on the door. Arnold made sure it was locked and looked through the peephole. It was Harry.

"There you are. I came by a while ago but no one answered, just some more of that infernal barking." Harry held his just-lit cigarette in his mouth as he spoke.

"I was robbed!" Arnold said. "Right outside the back gate, just now! And they hit me." He cupped his throbbing cheek in his hand.

"Jeezus, in broad daylight? Goddamn police don't keep any order around here. Better put some ice on that. Want the wife to take a look at it? She was a nurse back in the day. How much did they get off you?"

"Forty dollars. They tried to make me let them into my apartment, but I refused." Yes, he *had* stood up to the thieves, and they'd backed down. Or maybe they simply were on their way to another alley to see what the pickings might be.

"My leeks and arugula. And those new potatoes," he muttered.

"Huh? My man, are you OK? The wife could look in on you. Did you call the police?"

At least Harry knew what had happened to him and insisted that "the wife" check him. At least he wasn't lying bleeding or dead in the alley, with no one discovering him until the next day.

Other people, yes, one needs other people. You need a special person most of all, Arnold thought, to be by your side as you meet all the terrors as well as the joys of life, someone who knows of your comings and goings and cares about you.

"Maybe you need to go park yourself on the couch. The shock or something." Harry patted Arnold gently on the back. "Now you go get some rest."

Arnold called the police and checked the welt on his face. He dabbed some antibiotic cream on a small nick that was starting to ooze a drop of blood and covered the wound with a lozenge-shaped Band-Aid.

The police car wailed up to the front of the apartment five minutes later. The officers, a man and a woman, were not much older than his undergraduates.

When Arnold had described the two thugs, the male officer said, "Sounds like the ones who jumped someone in the park last night."

The cops poked around the backyard and the alley.

"We'll let you know if we catch up with them. Could happen. Doesn't sound like they're all that bright," the male officer said.

"Do you want to get that looked at?" The female officer rested her hand on the revolver on her slender hip as she peered at the Band-Aid on Arnold's face.

"Fortunately only a bruise and a small cut."

"OK. But you call your doctor if you spike a fever or it gets red."

Civil and thoughtful for a pair of cops, Arnold thought when they had left, though what they could or would actually do to nab his assailants was unclear. And they could not patch up his now glass-fragile sense of security. A feeling of exhaustion, starting with his face and spreading to his limbs, sent him to lie down on the couch, as Harry had prescribed. It was still just barely two o'clock. He could close his eyes for a few minutes and be up in plenty of time to get some more supplies at the Central Co-op before Laurel arrived at six.

This time he would go out the front door and hurry down the sidewalk to Madison, a busy street with plenty of Sunday pedestrians and not the territory of a blue-eyed creep and his sidekick.

Leroy's barking by the front door awoke Arnold.

"Hey, are you in there?"

Exasperated knocks.

"Hey, Arn. Last chance if you're in there. Can't you hear your dog? You said six o'clock."

Arnold sat up and ran his hands through his sweaty mussed hair, casting off an intense dream, something about Hamilton Dodge chasing him up the back alley. His throbbing cheek brought it all back to him: He had been robbed, hit in the face, had planned to take a short nap—but now it was past six o'clock.

"My apologies," he said as he pulled open the door and leaned down to quiet Leroy.

"Did you just get up from a nap? I thought you said come over at six. And what happened to your face?" She handed him a paper bag with a bottle of wine.

"It is a long story, as they say. If you would give me a moment?"

Laurel plopped down on the sofa while Arnold excused himself and ducked into the bathroom. The bruise was morphing into a multihued bulge. Arnold slipped into his bedroom and retrieved the clean black shirt from his closet. There would be no romantic tête-à-tête with candlelight, no comforting homemade potato leek soup or elegant French cakes. He would take her out, but that would mean sitting across from each other at a restaurant table as they had done already, not the evolution of intimacy he had hoped to help along by inviting her to his home.

And he had not had time to put away the plates and bowls in the dish drainer or wipe down the counters or scrub out the cast-iron skillet with its fried-egg bits.

"I'm looking for the corkscrew." Laurel rummaged in the drawer by the sink that held a stapler, a small sewing kit, various expired coupons, some thumbtacks and screws, and a tube of household glue, among other things.

How embarrassing, that she would see his disorganized junk drawer and messy kitchen!

Arnold quickly pulled the wine opener from the silverware drawer and opened her contribution of pinot grigio. He poured her a glass.

"So where did you get that shiner?" As Laurel leaned against the counter cradling her wineglass, Arnold flashed back to the image of Frieda Hamm, in her kitchen on the evening of the department party, so obviously trying to flirt with him.

He poured himself some wine, his hands trembling even as he heard his own casual reporting of the event.

"Wow. At least it wasn't any worse. They didn't pull a gun or anything?"

"They weren't *carrying*, as far as I could tell," Arnold said.

As Laurel leaned forward to inspect his swollen cheek, Arnold found himself starting to pull her into his arms. He reached behind him to put his wineglass on the kitchen counter, but he miscalculated and the glass toppled onto the floor.

"Whoa!" Laurel backed away from the splattered wine and shattered glass and honk-laughed.

"Pardon me," Arnold said as Leroy trotted into the kitchen to find out what might need hoovering off the kitchen floor. "No, *bad dog. Shoo!*" The chastened Leroy slunk away. Arnold snapped a fistful of paper towels off the dispenser by the sink and crouched down to mop up the mess.

Laughed. She had *laughed*. There he was, making a pass, but it had become a slapstick routine that made her laugh.

"Sorry, that wasn't cool to laugh, but it was sort of a Woody Allen moment." She tore off a paper towel.

Arnold's voice broke with a huge sob, and he dabbed his eyes with a fresh paper towel. "Pardon me. It has been a trying day. They reminded me that they know where I live."

"Hey, being mugged is horrible. I can't say it has happened to me, but I remember what it was like when someone stole stuff out of my car and took it for a joyride. They knew my address. I was freaked." Laurel moistened some paper towels. "Hey, I'll finish up."

As she got down on her hands and knees to scrub the tiles, Arnold recalled that she had taken the same position to inspect Gludger's smoke-soaked carpet. Her flowery scent mingled with the odor of the spilled wine. She understood what he was going through, though this was not the point of commonality he would have chosen.

Arnold excused himself to the bathroom and doused his face with cold water. I'll compose myself and suggest somewhere for dinner, he thought. We've both had some tough times the past couple of weeks, and we need each other's support. But when he returned to the living room, Laurel was by the front door, her leather bag slung over her shoulder.

"I think I got all the little bits of glass off the floor. You know, it's pretty clear you're not up for much this evening. I'm heading out."

"No worries. I'm feeling much better now and could use some Thai food. My treat." He squeezed her shoulder but, to his chagrin, she pulled away.

"Hey, sorry about what happened, but you need to chill tonight. Watch some TV or something. Another time, OK?"

Laurel offered an open half hug and was out the door.

Chapter Twenty-Five

On Monday Gardenia tried to master the heartache of Sylvie's upcoming move by spending the early June evening in the garden.

She spaded compost into her vegetable beds, weeded, and planted spinach and bush beans. While taking Susie for a walk, she stopped herself a half dozen times from checking for a message from Hans—it had now been more than two weeks since they'd talked. Returning home around eight she was famished, so she heated up a can of vegetarian baked beans and cut two thick slices from a day-old artisan loaf for toast.

I am like one of those excellent women in a Barbara Pym novel, she thought, bravely opening a tin for my solitary meal, my little dog waiting expectantly at my feet. Or maybe it should be a cat in my lap? I suppose I should have some potted meat as well, whatever that is.

Boldly she poured herself an IPA ale from the six-pack that had been languishing in the fridge since Hans's last visit. The bitter taste went well with the sweet beans and the crisp, thickly buttered toast. She had almost finished the ale and was considering opening another— she would drink only a tiny bit—when her cell phone pinged. Sylvie, apologizing again? she wondered.

That's not my boy. I won't let myself go there, she thought. Hopes down, hopes down.

But joy of joys, it was Hans. "Hi, Ma, coming over."

"Great!"

Gardenia emptied the rest of the ale down the kitchen drain and quickly scraped the leftover beans into an empty yogurt container and stuck it in the fridge. She had just combed her hair and brushed her teeth when Hans let himself in the front door.

Oh, my boy! She almost hurtled across the room into his arms but held back for fear of spooking him and also because he stood on the doormat not with an armful of radiant Milo but instead, a bulging duffel bag and backpack.

"Mom, I'll get right to the point. I need to move home for a while. Can I put this stuff in my old room?"

"Of course, of course."

"So what's up?" Gardenia said when he returned to the kitchen, hoping that she sounded casual.

He said, "Mom, it's not going to help me if you freak out, OK? So try not to. Caitlin and I are splitting up. She's been seeing somebody else. A guy she met on the bus, for Chrissakes. You were right. She acted like you were lying or totally paranoid or something when I asked her about being with a guy by the KFC. But last night she changed her story. She's 'in love.'"

"Oh, Hans, I am so sorry! I hoped and hoped that I was wrong, but at least now you know for sure." Gardenia hugged him. "At least we still have Milo."

"*We?* Oh please, don't make this about you, Mom." He pulled away from her. "As a matter of fact *we* may *not* have Milo, at least not now.

Caitlin took him to her parents' fuckin' place, and she won't answer my texts or pick up her phone. I mean fuck it all to hell—she's the one who was screwing someone else, so why do I get punished?"

Have I ever heard him swear like this? Gardenia wondered.

How tired Hans looked, how plain worn-out and desperately sad, with his unshaven face that was not an attempt at sexy élan but instead a manifestation of stress and sorrow.

"Have you had supper? I have some baked beans," Gardenia offered lamely.

"Oh, Mom, why would I want baked beans? I'm gonna take a shower."

Stupid me, why didn't I suggest a shower, *not* baked beans? she scolded herself.

After ten minutes, the shower was still on, full force.

He wouldn't, in his grief and rage, hurt himself?

"Hans, can I make you a grilled cheese sandwich?" she called from the other side of the bathroom door. "I have one of those ales you like. From the last time you were here."

"OK."

When Hans emerged from the bathroom he was clean-shaven and wearing a fresh T-shirt with his jeans. He poured ketchup on the plate for his grilled cheese and drank the ale straight from the bottle.

How young my son is, Gardenia thought, coming up on his twenty-fifth birthday. And yet how old he seems, a father and a provider and a thwarted talent and a cuckolded husband and soon to be part of a broken family.

Gardenia turned on the jazz radio station. Errol Garner, playing a complex piano solo.

"Oh man." Hans stood up and turned the volume higher. "That guy. I used to listen to him all the time. All I wanted to do was play like that."

"You still can. It's not too late."

"No, Mom, thanks for the vote of confidence, but it *is* too late. I'm going to go hang out in my room."

At least she had not weakened and asked him about all the horrid details that she did, and didn't, want to know.

Chapter Twenty-Six

Tuesday evening Gardenia's cell rang.

"Hi! Old-fashioned, to actually make a phone call, but I wanted to ask you to join me for a happy hour at Oceana. That place over by the canal."

Lex had emailed Gardenia a few days after the Cascade Ballroom date to say he would once again be out of town but would get in touch when he returned.

"I'm not sure," Gardenia said. "I had a long day at work." Which was not exactly true—finals were at the end of the week, and most of the English professors had cancelled classes. Not even Arnold and Leroy had shown up that day.

"Then you need a reward. Can I pick you up at seven?"

"Well, OK. But I'll meet you there."

After the startling experience with Bruce, Gardenia had no desire to sit in the front seat of a car with a man. She had no idea if Lex would pounce on her as Bruce had, but still. She would drive herself and play it safe.

Going out with Lex would give Hans a chance to have the house to himself, though she wouldn't tell him that she had a date. Better not to complicate Hans's life with any possible worry about his mother.

And better to err on the side of casual dress, she thought, just black pants and a white V-necked T-shirt with a brown cashmere cardigan. In a nod to the bistro aspect of Oceana, she chose a silk scarf and tried to tie it as a Parisienne might and not so that it looked like a fancy bandage.

"Good to see you." Lex was waiting by the maître d's podium and greeted her with a side-by-side hug.

She felt that jolt of attraction again, not quite welcome but not unwelcome either.

The server found them a table on the deck, with a view of the far side of the canal and the row of poplar trees with pale green baby leaves.

"See that building on the other side of the canal? The one with the metal sculptures on the facade? I helped the artist figure out how to hang them. More weight than a façade should have to manage, but it worked. The architect even remembered to mention my name as the engineer when it got an article in the *Seattle Times*."

"Cool," Gardenia said but her attention veered to a family of five sitting at the table behind Lex, a couple with their baby and a set of grandparents. They were laughing and chatting loudly, in a foreign language. French? The young father sat beside his mother—it was obvious that they belonged to each other, with the same round faces and dark wavy hair. The mother-in-law leaned across the table and squeezed the young wife's hand and said something to her with animated facial expressions. They both flung their heads back and laughed at whatever was funny.

"*Hello?*" Lex said.

"Sorry. I was watching that family. Trying to catch what they were saying. I mean, what language they were speaking. Must be French?" But I'm thinking about how happy some families are, she thought. I'm wondering why I can't be having a jolly supper on a June evening with my son and husband and grandchild and a cheerful, appreciative daughter-in-law.

Lex said, "Yep, it's French. I go to Paris now and then. I have a friend from college who lives there. This place reminds me of France, even though the food isn't strictly French."

"I wouldn't know, I've never been there," Gardenia said. "But I came here with a friend once, for lunch. We imagined we were sitting at some café with a view of the Seine. We drank wine, which I usually don't do in the middle of the day. We had to kill some time before I was sober enough to drive us home." She and Sylvie had laughed and laughed over their cheese plate and salad and glasses of house red, feeling tipsy and lighthearted as they sat in the warm noontime sun.

"Ah yes, we Americans are so fussy about drinking and driving. The French drink wine with a meal and drive home, never think it's a big deal." Lex winked, as if he thought Gardenia would agree that this was some clever naughtiness.

"I don't think that's a good idea, if you want to know the truth."

"Well, maybe it isn't, but there you have it. May I suggest the mussels as a starter?" Lex said. "And just *one* glass of wine. Since we have to drive home." He winked again.

As Lex and Gardenia silently pried bits of mussel flesh from the shells, the Happy Family was softly crooning to the baby and patting their hands together in a rhythm game. The mother-in-law caught the daughter-in-law's eye and smiled, as if to say, "Look at what a wonderful child you made for us!"

"Hey, I must be missing a good show," Lex said as the server set a salad in front of each of them. "You keep watching those people. I mean, I don't claim to be the most fascinating conversationalist, but still."

"Sorry," Gardenia said. "They are having such a good time."

The French grandparents and daughter-in-law smiled with delight as the young father spooned some chocolate gelato into the baby's mouth.

Gardenia heard herself say, "They're splitting up."

"What? Who?"

"My son and his wife."

"Whoa."

"All the custody issues. Even though *she* cheated, she thinks she should have Milo most of the time. And her parents are rich enough to hire fancy lawyers."

"Ah well. Maybe not the worst thing if the dad has joint custody. Your son is pretty young, isn't he? He'll be wanting to get back in circulation, right? A kid to take care of isn't the most seductive accessory." Lex tore a piece of baguette into two surprisingly equal-sized chunks and dunked them in the pot liquor. He pointed at a white yacht that was skimming under the Fremont Bridge. "Now what is it that people do to get themselves a setup like that?"

"Wait. Wait. Don't talk about yachts!" Gardenia snapped. "Let's go back to what you were saying about Hans not wanting to take care of his son. You are wrong. You are so, *so* wrong. You're not a parent, you have no idea how it feels to be separated from a child."

"Guess that sounded kind of flip. You're right, I don't know how it feels. I was just trying to help you see a bright side."

"Frankly you don't know the first thing about any of this." Gardenia slapped a twenty-dollar bill and a five on the table. "That's for my share. I can't do this, sorry."

"Hey, Gardenia, aren't you a little sensitive? I get that divorces are hard, but things tend to work out, in my experience."

"Yes, I'm sensitive. I *am* sensitive and I take things seriously because... because... because I'm a *mother!*"

Happy Family paused from the gelato feeding and watched Gardenia hurry toward the Oceana front door.

Her car was parked near the restaurant, but she slipped quickly around the side of the building and toward the Fremont Bridge. She would kill time somewhere in Fremont and cross back over to her car later, after Lex had given up and gone home.

I'll run, Gardenia thought, or at least walk as fast as I can. But she had forgotten about the uneven pavement on the Fremont Bridge pedestrian path. The toe of one shoe caught the edge of a rough seam, and she stumbled, breaking her fall with her hands.

"Are you OK?" A young male cyclist in a helmet stopped and peered down at her. "Can you get up? Or wait, maybe you shouldn't get up?"

"I'm OK. I'm pretty sure I'm OK." Blood was oozing from the scraped skin on her palms.

"Here, let me help you." He dismounted and held his hands out to her as if inviting her to do a schottische. "Why don't you lean against the railing here for a minute? Luckily I didn't make things worse by running right over you. Can I call someone for you?"

"I wish you could call my husband," Gardenia said, "but you can't. He's dead."

The young man blinked. "I'm sorry to hear that."

"Thank you. I have a son, about your age, but his life is a mess. My life is kind of a mess. Well, not completely, but it's confusing. I mean I have a lot to be thankful for. Like not breaking my neck when I fell. Sometimes a woman is going down the basement stairs to put laundry in the washer, and she slips and breaks her hip and her life is changed forever!"

"I'd suggest that you sit down somewhere for a while," the cyclist said.

"I'm OK. Thank you for stopping. I'd like to call your mother and compliment her on raising you right."

"Oh, anyone would do the same." He offered Gardenia his water bottle. "Please. I haven't drunk from this yet today."

The cool water tasted good after the salty mussels, and she finished nearly half the bottle. "Why is it that in crisis situations, people are always offered something to drink?" she asked. "It's always tea or whiskey or brandy. Sometimes water. Never milk."

"Heh heh," the young man replied as she handed back the water bottle.

"The way life can change in a second!" she said. "People dying of heart attacks, and cheating on their husbands, and friends moving away."

"You're sure there's no one I can call?" The cyclist looked at her with concern.

Maybe you knocked something loose in your head, is what he's thinking, Gardenia thought, wondering herself at her stream-of-consciousness prattle.

"No, I'm all right. Thank you for stopping. You are a kind person."

"All right. But take care." He looked back twice as he rode away and waved. He's hoping I don't leap over the bridge railing, Gardenia thought.

She watched her step as she crossed the bridge and walked as fast as she could up Fremont Avenue.

I'll compose an apologetic email to Lex and let him know that I'm not interested in seeing him again, Gardenia thought. He'll reply coldly or not at all. Hey, I could give him Dr. Laurel DuBarr's email address. The two of them seemed to have something to talk about at Frieda's party.

The June evening was stretching out toward nine o'clock as the early summer wended its way toward the longest day of the year. I'm not ready to go home yet, Gardenia thought. Remembering the Happy Family and the baby, she decided to have a gelato and used the last six dollars in her wallet to buy two scoops, coconut and pistachio, from the shop near the Lenin statue.

How Hans had loved to come to Fremont when he was in grade school. The three of them—a Happy Family—had made the rounds of all the sculptures in the neighborhood, though Hans was frightened of the Troll underneath the Aurora Bridge.

That's where I'll go to eat my gelato, she decided. The Troll was the same as she remembered, not defaced by graffiti and with his hub-cap eye shining as he clutched the Volkswagen Beetle under his claw of a left hand. No wonder Hans had been scared of this creation.

We'll bring Milo to see the Troll someday, maybe when he's ten or so, Gardenia thought. No need to add any scary images to his world.

A gaily laughing group joined her by the Troll while she was finishing the last tiny spoonful of gelato.

It was the Happy Family, taking a stroll after their frolicsome dinner. The grandmother cradled the baby while the daughter-in-law hung affectionately on her arm. They chattered away in French and took turns posing for a photo in front of the Troll, the cosseted baby not frightened at all in the arms of his joyous *grand-mère*.

Chapter Twenty-Seven

GARDENIA WAS AMAZED that Daddy Curlew offered to pay for the piano movers, without being asked. On Wednesday two burly guys about Hans's age shoved the old upright into its familiar corner in the living room.

"He's going to list the condo for rent already," Hans sneered. "Didn't want any of our stuff in there past today. Couldn't wait to cash in on some empty real estate. Like it wasn't our home for all those months and maybe we needed to think about it."

Gardenia was surprised to hear Hans say *our* and *we*. "I suppose there is some instinctive reaction when a real estate agent sees an empty dwelling. He gets an urge to put people in it. Like the sound of running water makes a beaver want to build a dam."

She thought her analogy clever but Hans just said, "Whatever."

That evening, when Gardenia went to the basement to start a load of laundry, she heard Hans talking on the phone upstairs. From the tone of his voice, she guessed it was Caitlin: first a flat, noncommittal string of words, followed by agitation, even anger, and before he hung up, a neutral, almost civil comment of some sort.

"Mom, I can go get Milo!"

Hans's face shone with an open joy Gardenia had not seen for ages. Weeks? Months? Since he had started living with Caitlin? He pulled off his tired white T-shirt and put on a clean one with a logo for a Thai beer.

"Should I go with you?"

"Naw, not a good idea. I'll go by myself. Better start getting some practice, picking up my son. She wants me to take him for the rest of the week. And the weekend." Hans hugged Gardenia. "Hey, Mom, by the way—sorry I didn't pick up or text you after you told me about Caitlin at the KFC. I wanted you to be wrong."

"That's OK. If you can switch to night shifts this week, I'll take over with Milo when you go to work."

"Thanks. But tomorrow I have to go in early."

"No worries. I'll call my boss and ask for the day off. Arnold will understand."

Arnold had shared his cell number with her. When he picked up, his voice sounded unusually flat.

"Arnold? It's Gardenia. I need to ask for the day off tomorrow. A family situation."

"Ah. That is no problem."

"Thanks. Are you OK? You sound like something's going on."

Silence.

"Arnold?"

"Indeed, one could say something is *going on*. I was mugged on Sunday. Several days ago, but I am sorry to say it has brought me low, as the saying goes. I am grateful that I am not required to teach this week. I doubt that I would give a stellar performance."

"I am so sorry. Did they hurt you?"

"A facial bruise. And they managed to take only forty dollars. But one's sense of security does get a good shaking up, doesn't it?"

"How about if I drop by? Maybe you need some company."

Gardenia didn't expect Arnold to agree, but he said without pause, "Thank you, I would be most grateful."

When Arnold opened the door, the air in the apartment was fusty, as if he had not opened his windows for several days despite the fresh early-summer air. The coffee table held empty Chinese takeout containers and the plastic trays used for ready-made sushi. The teapot, swathed in its hand-knit cozy, sat on the kitchen table.

"I was about to pour myself a cuppa," he said, stroking his unshaven face. "Won't you join me?"

"Well, thank you."

Sitting stiffly on a dining chair with her mug of tea, since settling into the easy chair or onto the sofa might imply that she was going to stay for a longer visit, she said, "It's a big deal, getting robbed. A kind of loss. Losing that sense of safety."

"A small loss compared to what many endure," Arnold said. "The loss of your husband, for example. From what my mother says, the grief never goes away."

"That's right. It's amazing what people will say. Like you're supposed to forget about it and not bother them anymore. They don't like to see you sad. It's boring or something. They don't want to talk about it either. You're thinking about him night and day and they won't even say his name."

"His name was Torre, I believe you mentioned?"

"That's right. Torre."

They switched from Keemun to some fizzy hard cider that Gardenia had brought in a canvas bag, thinking that this beverage bridged the gap between hot milky drinks and alcohol.

Arnold recounted what had happened in the alley, and Gardenia listened.

Gardenia talked about Torre and Hans and Milo, and Arnold listened.

Arnold didn't bring up Laurel, the petition, or the prospect of teaching freshmen how to compose a decent paragraph.

If fate had handed him English comp, he would *deal*, Gardenia thought, as Hans might say. When it came right down to it, what other option was there in life? You have to deal. Everyone does. I have my widowhood and my worries about Hans with his failed marriage and delayed music career. Laurel has her string of adjunct jobs. Frieda has her unrequited love for Arnold Wiggens. Dorothy Wiggens has the sorrow of no grandchildren. All human beings deal, in one way or another, until they die.

That's why all those Chaucer pilgrims wanted to tell their stories, she thought. Lost in their narrations, they could forget about whatever form of dealing awaited.

And through it all, we remain who we are, Gardenia thought. Even as life makes us deal, we are always ourselves.

"You know, I think we need to go outside for a while. Fresh air helps. Even though it's starting to rain," she said. "I heard the weather report, so I wore my rain jacket."

Arnold ran his hand through his uncombed curls.

"I suppose I should clean up," he said.

"Naw. No one on the Hill cares."

Arnold pulled his rain jacket from a coatrack next to the front door. "It's still light out, so I'll give you the theology tour of the neighborhood," he said. "A different church on every corner. Even onion domes, perhaps concealing petunias."

In a few weeks Dr. Laurel DuBarr would be on her way, spending the summer with the final editing of her book of opaque prose and moving on to another adjunct job. Frieda Hamm would be off on her much-touted trip to Oregon. Arnold would figure out how to make English comp bearable for him and the students. And fingers crossed that he finds a publisher for his book, Gardenia thought.

As the administrative assistant, I don't have a summer break, she reminded herself, so I'll be at my desk, taking care of whatever department business comes up. Hans will be staying with me, and sometimes precious Milo. I'll ask if I can bring Susie to the office with me. Arnold and I can take the dachshunds for a walk around campus. And I'll invite him and Leroy to join Susie and me for Saturday morning visits to the *small, shy, and elderly* corral in the dog park.

Arnold put on his rain jacket. He followed Gardenia down the stairs and once outside, they both put up their hoods.

"*The rain is raining all around, / It falls on field and tree*," Gardenia began.

"*It rains on the umbrellas here, / And on the ships at sea*," Arnold finished.

"Except everyone knows that hardly anyone in Seattle uses an umbrella," Gardenia said.

"Indeed."

And although Gardenia knew it was not at all appropriate for an acting department chair to be so forward with the administrative assistant, she did not resist when Arnold took her hand and kissed the back of it in thanks.

Acknowledgments

I AM DEEPLY GRATEFUL to Robin Cruise for her fastidious, perceptive, and good-humored editing of the manuscript—skilled editors are akin to angels. Many thanks too to Dianne Aprile and Linda Dailey, who offered valuable comments on an earlier version of the manuscript, and to Phyllis DeBlanche for careful proofreading.

Fay Jones, Jon Jory, Mercedes Lawry, Michiyo Morioka, and Linda Shaw kindly agreed to write letters of recommendation for grant applications. My delightful Book Club members—Sandra Chait, Linda Dailey, Isabel Hamilton, Carol Hermer, Juliana Heyne, Ann Horwitt, Fay Jones, and Sondra Shulman—have introduced me to dozens of fine books. Margaret Allen has offered loyal friendship and encouragement since we met in 1975. Linda Dailey has been a constant friend and cheerleader for thirty-five years, a true blessing in my life. My sons, Andrew and Colin, are role models for me in their focused pursuit of their artistic and career goals. Emily Painter and Lois Hanson, my excellent sisters, boosted my confidence with their enthusiasm for the manuscript. My brother-in-law, Geert Glas, gave useful legal advice.

Financial support from my dear mother, Rebecca Hanson, enabled me to move forward with publication.

A generous grant from the Elizabeth George Foundation gave me precious time for my writing projects. A heartfelt thank-you to Mitchell S. Waters of Curtis Brown, Ltd., for believing in me and this novel. Kathy Campbell of Gorham Printing contributed her fine design skills.

I dedicate *Always Gardenia* with love to my husband, who for more than thirty-seven years has supported my writing ambitions in ways large and small. I am a lucky woman.

Made in the USA
Monee, IL
15 July 2023